Praise for *Makai Queen*

"*Makai Queen* has a way of instantly inviting the reader into a story, or rather an adventure with the added excitement of the unknown! You will find yourself scrambling from page to page wondering what's going to happen next. I highly recommend *Makai Queen* for anyone seeking to join this risky adventure."

NATE LANZON, YOUTH PASTOR, CENTRAL CHRISTIAN CHURCH, MESA, AZ

"Makai Queen provides a new twist in the young adult market, blending action and suspense with a message of virtue and truth to a generation that is searching. Don't pass it up!"

TIM WIMBERLY, PASTOR OF FAMILY MINISTRIES,
CHURCH OF LIVING WATER, OLYMPIA WA

"Tara Fairfield, in her wonderful novel, *Makai Queen*, makes finding the perfect balance between realistic reactions and feelings, and imaginary situations that occur in the majestic undersea haven of Moku-Ola, seem effortless."

CHELSEA, AGE THIRTEEN.

"Follow the incredible story of Tessa Armstrong as she enters an amazing world in which she unexpectedly discovers her destiny as well as her Creator. From the very first chapter, author Tara Fairfield takes you into an action-packed story in a world of creative beauty. Tara's vivid imagination, coupled with an engaging story, draws the reader into a world of unique characters, tremendous places, and a plot filled with surprises, twists, and turns, which all conspire to keep the reader absorbed in a colorful world of make believe . . . or is it?"

DON LAWRENCE, PASTOR, CHRIST CHURCH OF FOUNTAIN HILLS,
FOUNTAIN HILLS, AZ

MAKAI QUEEN

TARA FAIRFIELD

Deep River
B O O K S

Published by
Deep River Books
Sisters, Oregon
www.deepriverbooks.com

ISBN-10: 19377560X
ISBN-13: 9781937756703

Library of Congress: 2012954325
Printed in the USA

Cover design by David Litwin, Purefusion Media

Dedicated to
Ashley, Tyler, and Alyssa
You inspire me each and every day!
and
Praise, honor, and glory to my heavenly Father.

*For we are his workmanship, created in Christ Jesus for good works,
which God prepared beforehand, that we should walk in them.*
Ephesians 2:10

PROLOGUE

I stood on the bow of a great ship, leaning over the railing to look down into the dark water. A shadowy form rose below me, slowly taking the shape of a man. When he broke the surface, I saw his face. He had deep, dark eyes and long black hair. His skin shone golden in the moonlight.

Something stirred below, and I forced my eyes back to the water. From even deeper, another shape began to emerge; larger, fiercer, and not human. My body froze, goose bumps creeping down my spine. A red cloud spread out beneath the shape.

CHAPTER 1

KAMOHOALI'I

Life doesn't play nice. It isn't fair. If a happily ever after existed, I was pretty sure it had taken a left turn off the road I was on. I exhaled, letting my body grow heavy, tension evaporating from every pore. The rhythm of the waves washing up onshore lulled me into a daze. Surf pooled around my feet, creating caverns beneath my heels. My toes wiggled deep into the sand as the last rays of sun warmed my face. Time to head home, but I didn't move, greedily inhaling the salty, moist air. The peace of the ocean called to me like an old friend.

I knew I'd have to face Rachel sooner or later. Her lectures were inevitable. She had strong views on my life and how I needed to get it together. With reluctance, I got up and trudged toward my car. Something shiny down the beach at the edge of the water caught my eye. I jogged over to get a closer look. Any opportunity to put off facing Rachel was worth taking. A man lay passed out on the sand, legs floating in the shallow surf. My heart raced—there was no one else on the beach, and I had no clue how to do CPR. I grabbed his arms and dragged him up onto the beach. I put my head to his chest and checked to see if he was breathing.

The soft wheeze of air going in and out of his lungs told me he was alive. I let out a breath I didn't know I was holding, relieved no CPR was needed. I drew back on my heels to check him out. He was wearing a silver wetsuit from the waist down that sparkled in the twilight. He was huge, at least six foot four, and muscular—there was no fat on this guy. A strange mark stood out on his chest right over his heart, not a birthmark but not like any tattoo I'd seen before either. A shark surrounded by strange symbols.

I grabbed his shoulders and shook him, hoping to wake him up. He didn't respond. Maybe it was time to call for help. This was definitely out of my league. I leaned closer and pulled the phone out of my pocket. He opened his eyes. My heart leaped into my throat, and I froze.

"Do I look dead?" His voice held a tinge of humor.

I shook my head. Was he making fun of me? My stomach did a flip. "Maybe a little."

He smiled up at me. "Seriously, you look terrified. I give you my word, I'm not a sea monster." Hmmm . . . he kinda looked like one. His hair was sleek and black, reaching down to his waist. His eyes were dark, almost black. He didn't look much older than I was, but something about him seemed ancient, or maybe scary. Something was off. He reminded me of someone.

I recovered my voice and asked, "Are you okay? I thought you'd drowned." I stuck my hands in my pockets to hide their shaking. It hit me why he looked familiar. He looked like the guy in my dream, but that couldn't be right—dreams aren't real.

He sat up, shaking sand from his hair. "No, just a little weak. I'll be okay." He looked up and down the beach as though checking for something. His jaw clenched, and he seemed edgy. "What are you doing out here alone?"

Heat rose in my face. "Excuse me, but you're the one being pulled out of the water," I snapped. I turned and looked behind me. There was nobody anywhere on the beach. Nobody to hear me if I needed to scream for help. I shuddered. Maybe Rachel was right, maybe I shouldn't have come out here alone. I eased back away from him.

He laughed. "Sorry, I didn't mean to offend you. Honestly I'm grateful."

The knot in my throat relaxed a little, and I smiled back at him. "Do you need me to call anyone?"

He shook his head. "No, I'm fine."

"You don't look fine. You're covered in sand, you have circles under your eyes, and you have no transportation back to wherever you came from. Oh, and what are you doing swimming alone out here, anyway? Everyone on the islands knows not to venture into the water alone. My brother-in-law tells me there are sharks off this beach." The shaking in my hands stopped, and my confidence returned. I wanted him to know I had family in the area. I wasn't totally alone.

"I'm sorry, I've been rude. May I ask your name so I can thank you properly for coming to help me?"

I squinted at him. Was he serious, or did he just age about twenty years? I went with it. "I'm Tessa, Tessa Armstrong." I offered him my hand and he took it.

"Hi, Tessa, my name is Ka moho-alii, but most people call me Moho."

"Moho?" That name sounded familiar. "Do you know my brother-in-law, Mike Hale?"

His lips drew together. "No, don't know any Mike Hale."

He tugged on my hand, drawing me closer. His warm breath caressed my cheek. A shudder went through me. I pulled my hand out of his grasp and jumped back to put some distance between us. His eyes locked onto mine, intense, piercing. The heat rose in my cheeks again, but I couldn't look away. Alarm bells went off in my head, and

I could hear my sister Rachel saying, "Don't go to isolated places with men you don't know."

He jumped to his feet and extended his hand to me. "Can I walk you to your car?"

I paused. He hadn't made any move to hurt me. He seemed harmless enough, so I reached up and took his hand. "Sure, I'm parked just down the beach." My voice cracked and I looked away, hoping he hadn't noticed. I stood up and resolved to gain control of myself, my mind racing. I looked back at him. "What happened to you? Why were you on the beach like that?"

He hesitated, looking up and down the beach again. "I swam a long distance and needed to rest."

Okay, that was vague. I took a deep breath. "What do you mean, you needed to rest? You were swimming between the islands alone, weren't you?" He was either an insanely strong swimmer or just insane. "Where were you going? Is someone going to pick you up or at least tracking you? Do you need a ride?"

He looked at me and raised an eyebrow. "Wow, that's a lot of questions." He laughed.

I narrowed my eyes and waited.

"No, I don't need a ride, but I appreciate the offer." He jerked his head, motioning down the beach. "Walk with me."

I took a step away from him.

He chuckled.

Every muscle in my body tensed. I folded my arms across my chest and squared off on him, looking him straight in the eye.

He sighed. "A few months ago my father was killed, leaving my mother alone and very weak. Two weeks ago, my mother, Hiiaka, and my best friend, Kele, were kidnapped. I've been searching for them but haven't been able to find them."

Before I could respond, a low, throaty growl rose up from behind me. I whirled, hands forward.

With one quick movement, Moho was in front of me, blocking my view. I tried to peer around him, but he was so large, it was difficult to see. I slid to the side to get a better look.

Less than two feet away stood the scariest crocodile I'd ever seen. Rows and rows of teeth lined up in the thing's mouth. Its tail was bigger than my car. As I sucked in a ragged gasp, thoughts raced through my brain. Since when did crocodiles live on Lanai?

Moho glared at the crocodile and in a low voice said, "No, Kupua, you will not take her." He turned, grabbed me by the waist, and plunged us both into the surf. Cold water rushed up my nose, stinging my throat. I screamed and started kicking him. I clawed at his arms, but he only grunted and shoved us deeper into the water. My mouth filled with the taste of salt, so I closed it. Tears welled up in my eyes. This guy was crazy. He was going to kill us both. I'd never see Rachel again.

Moho had both arms locked around me, crushing my back tight against his chest. I couldn't move. The water got colder and darker. What was he thinking? I struggled against him. Water rushed past my face. I would take scary crocodiles over drowning any day. I closed my eyes and conserved energy just in case there was a chance I could get away from this lunatic.

My sister's face flashed in my mind. Things weren't right between us. I'd always looked up to my big sis, but since our parents' deaths, things were different. A car accident took both Mom and Dad when I was only thirteen. Rachel and I'd clung to each other in our grief. We drew strength from each other. In the aftermath of our loss, she changed from my friend to my caretaker. It wasn't an easy transformation for either of us. Obedience wasn't my strong point. Truth was,

Rachel had done right by me. Now I might never get to tell her how much she really meant to me, how much I loved her.

I snuck a peek at my kidnapper and realized I wasn't drowning. In fact, I was breathing just fine. How could this be real?

A fissure in the ocean floor loomed below us. Moho headed straight for it. I closed my eyes again, muscles tensing. The walls of the fissure scraped my legs as we went through. I opened my eyes but couldn't see a thing. We were in a vast black sea. Cold cut through me, causing shivers to run up and down my spine. Bubbles popped and churned around us. All hope slipped away.

I went limp in Moho's arms, and his grip loosened. I didn't even think of escape now—there was no way I could get back to the surface on my own. A light shone ahead; a small tunnel. Moho swam into the opening, and we emerged through the surface into an underwater cave. Light emanated from the rock walls, and a sweet, musty scent filled the air. Moho lifted me out of the water and dropped me on the gravel ledge.

My legs collapsed underneath me. I lay on the gravel, shaking, water dripping down my face. Salt stung my eyes as I fought back tears. My lungs gulped air greedily. Slowly, I got my feet under me and stood up. I lifted my chin, drew back my shoulders, and faced Moho, voice trembling.

I drew back my fist and punched his chest hard. It was like hitting rock; he didn't budge. "Are . . . you . . . crazy? What do you think you're doing?"

He looked down his nose at me. "Saving your life," he replied, "but we have to keep moving." He grabbed my wrist and yanked me down into a lava tube.

I tried to twist my arm out of his grip, shouting, "Saving my life? Are you crazy? Throwing me into the sea with a crocodile on the loose is saving my life? Oh, and while we're at it, why didn't I drown? Can you explain that to me, please?"

He ignored me and kept pulling me down the tunnel.

Enough was enough. I pulled back and slammed my foot into the back of his knee.

He crumpled with a thud and released his grip on my wrist. "Why did you do that?"

I huffed. "Well, now you're talking to me, aren't you? Some answers need to come my way before I go anywhere else with you." I gave a silent thank-you to my father for teaching me basic self-defense.

He shrugged. "Listen, I know you're upset and have a lot of questions. If you come with me, I'll explain everything."

I narrowed my eyes at him. "How about you explain now, and then take me back to the surface." I cringed at the thought of going back through that crack with him, but I had no choice. I clenched my fists and considered hitting him again.

He turned to face me but stayed on his knees. "Tessa, you have to believe me, it's not safe to go back. That crocodile is in the water looking for us. Until we get to my home, we will not be safe. Do you really want to take that chance?"

I shook my head at him. "I can't stay here. I need to get home. I don't care what's out there, take me home. Now." I stomped my foot. My voice echoed off the walls.

"Look, Tessa, I'm trying to help you, not hurt you. I promise after we make sure it's safe, I'll take you home. I have a lot to explain, so let's get somewhere safe."

I was so tempted to kick him again. But really, what good would it do? Maybe he was right about the crocodile. Maybe I was safer with him. That was a scary thought. I looked over my shoulder in case the crocodile had followed us. I nodded my head and resigned myself to moving forward. That was my motto, after all.

Moho got up and headed down the tunnel with a slight limp. I smiled and gave myself a pat on the back.

An eerie glow permeated the tunnel, reminding me of those glow sticks I used as a kid on Halloween. There was just enough illumination coming off the walls that I could see where to put my feet. Shadows hardened the lines on Moho's face, causing him to look older, crueler. Once in a while my eyes caught movement in the shadows of the crevices in the wall. The sound of little feet scurrying against the rock made my skin crawl. I kept close behind Moho.

He gradually picked up the pace. My muscles stretched and groaned as I lengthened my stride. I reached back and twisted my hair into a knot to keep it out of my face. I was used to running on the beach, and the sand under my feet felt like home. After several turns and at least two miles, we came to a massive door. I bent over with my hands on my knees to catch my breath. The door was carved out of rock. Ornate symbols like the one on Moho's chest swirled around the edges in circular patterns. There were words written above them, but they were in a language I didn't understand. I glared at Moho. My stomach warred with my brain. It felt like a blender was going off in my intestines. My gut didn't want to go into this guy's house, but my brain knew he was right about the crocodile. My brain also reminded me I couldn't swim home alone.

He looked down at me, hunger in his eyes. "This is the private entrance to my home." He pulled my hand up to the door and placed my palm next to his in the center. The door rumbled open.

CHAPTER 2

MOKU-OLA
ISLAND OF HEALING

Moho stepped across the threshold with me following close behind, stomach churning but head held high. Two men stood guard, heads bowed. Each wore baggy green pants with no shirt. We walked past them, and my feet slipped, forcing me to look down. Abalone shell covered the floor. Translucent blue and green shone through its clear surface. It felt smooth as glass under my bare feet. The walls and ceiling were the same volcanic rock as the tunnel and cast a soft light throughout the room. It was so quiet, I could hear my own ragged breath as I recovered from the run down the tunnel. Several sofas were positioned in a circle in the center of the room.

Moho motioned for me to sit on one of the sofas and instructed the guards to bring water. He wasn't winded at all from the run. He couldn't have been more than a year or two older than me, but he sure was in better shape. The guards never looked up, just walked out of the room, heads down. Moho's eyes followed them until they were gone. He looked back at me, face void of emotion but his eyes sharp as a hawk tracking its prey. "I'll be right back," he told me, and then he left the room.

I let out a deep breath and plopped down on a sofa, letting my head fall against the back cushion. Tears threatened to well up, but I fought them back and considered my options for getting out of there. It was obvious I wasn't going to be able to swim home without help. The two guards didn't look like they were gonna be much help either. They wouldn't even look at me.

I covered my face with my hands and took a few deep breaths. Rachel must have the whole city out searching for me by now. Did she think I was dead? The thought of her having to face the loss of another family member stung deep. She didn't deserve that; no one did. My heart felt ripped in half.

I dropped my hands and looked around the room. Where was I anyway, and why had he brought me here? Never, even in my wildest imagination, did I consider there might be people living under the ocean. This was unreal. I pinched myself just to be sure I wasn't dreaming. My arm stung. Nope, not dreaming. I sighed—too bad, at least I could've woken up from a dream.

Moho came back in, wearing loose-fitting khaki-colored drawstring pants and a pullover shirt. His black hair was pulled into a ponytail. He smiled at me.

I pulled my legs up onto the sofa and wrapped my arms around them, curling into a ball. He didn't look like he was about to chop me into little pieces with an ax, but I wasn't sure. He shoved some clothing at me and pointed to a doorway.

"Get out of those wet clothes, then we can talk." He was almost as bossy as Rachel, even though he looked much younger.

I uncurled, took the clothes, and closed the door behind myself, grateful for a few minutes alone. The gurgling in my stomach calmed.

The room was small, just a cushioned bench to sit on and a basket in the corner. Not really a bathroom, just a space to change clothes. Guess they did that a lot around here.

Shivering, I peeled off my wet, clinging clothes and dumped them in the corner. I pulled on a pair of plain yellow drawstring pants and T-shirt. The fabric felt soothing against my skin, warming my goose bumps away. Fashion never was my thing; I was into comfort, and these were the softest clothes I'd ever worn.

Nowhere near ready to go back and face Moho and his craziness, I pressed my back against the wall and slid to my knees. My head dropped into my hands, every inch of me shaking.

"Get a grip, Tessa, you can't fall apart now," I told myself. When I was safe at home, then I could allow myself the luxury of a breakdown, but now I needed to be strong. *What I wouldn't give for some of Rachel's advice.* Her usual bossiness didn't seem so bad right about now. I hadn't appreciated much about my life, but boy, what I wouldn't give to have it back right now. I shook myself. Time to get a grip. I got to my feet, lifted my chin, and stepped out of the room.

Back in the sitting room, a pitcher of water and two glasses had arrived. I settled into one of the sofas and poured myself a drink. The cool water soothed my parched throat and washed the lingering taste of salt from my mouth. I licked my lips and looked Moho in the eye. "Okay, we're here, we're safe. It's time for you to tell me what's going on."

He held out his arms. "This place, my home, is called Moku-ola, an island of life below the sea floor. We live in peace here, but because we sometimes travel to the surface, we have inspired legends among your people. You may have heard some?"

I nodded, thinking of the stories Mike's brother Puna had told me when I first arrived in Hawaii.

Puna often spoke of the story of Pele and her older brother, the shark god. The legend was that Pele's brother built her a canoe for her journey to Hawaii. He sometimes appeared in the form of a shark, and Pele would ride his back in the surf. Although he was good to Pele, the shark god was vicious, and stories were told of him killing and eating unsuspecting villagers. The blender went off in my stomach again as I wondered if Moho was a killer too.

Hunger returned to Moho's eyes. "My mother is the queen of my people. In Moku-ola, one person cannot rule alone. That power is too much for just one person to handle, and so a couple must share it. The crown is always given to the daughter, and special gifts are given to the sons. My parents didn't have any daughters, only two sons. When my father died, it left us vulnerable. A monster called Kupua took my mother and my friend Kele while they were outside the city in the ocean. He seeks power. Kupua can become any fish, reptile, bird, or mammal of the ocean. Some people say he has a special gift, but I know the truth. He only wants to take Moku-ola from me. At first I thought Kupua meant to harm my mother so he could claim her place, but now I believe he has a different plan." He looked at me, his face distorted and red.

There was silence as I sat waiting for him to explain. Sweat beaded on my brow until I couldn't take it anymore. "What do you mean, what does he plan to do?"

He leaned forward, his voice a growl. "He plans to take you."

Huh? I shook my head at him. "What could he possibly want with me? I didn't even know this place existed until you brought me here, and I'm not really lovin' the experience."

Moho snorted. "He has my mother because she is the only one who can name the new queen, passing on her power to the next generation."

I crossed my legs and leaned forward. "So? What does that have to do with me? I'm not one of you." *Was this guy for real? Did he really believe this story?*

His eyes blazed. "Each of us has one partner, a perfect match created for the other. Our partner is created for us at birth, and when the time is right will be revealed to us. When the queen has no daughters, the firstborn son's partner always comes from outside of our people, a new queen to join with us. Tessa, you are that chosen queen—it is your destiny, the Creator's plan for your life."

The room began to spin. I grabbed the arm of the couch to steady myself and stood up. I pointed my finger at him, voice trembling. "You are out of your mind. I am no queen, and I'm certainly not interested in being your partner. Take me home right now!"

The walls closed in on me. I felt trapped. My lungs heaved and gasped for air. Pulsating black dots filled my vision. I wrapped my arms around myself and bent over to keep from passing out.

Moho stood up and put his hands on my shoulders, steadying me. "What I'm saying is true, Tessa. You must accept your destiny. It's not safe for you out there right now. You are safe here, and you must stay until Kupua is caught."

No way was I going to stay, but how was I going to get out of this crazy place? I felt like Alice when she fell through the rabbit hole. If only there was a pill I could take to make it all go away. I stood there, shaking my head back and forth, my eyes closed against the black dots, unable to get any words out of my throat.

Moho whispered in my ear, "It's late. Sleep here, and tomorrow we can talk more, and I'll show you the city. If, after that, you still want to go home, I'll take you." He sounded way too sure of himself. This guy didn't understand the meaning of no.

I put my hands over my face, icy fingers cooling my burning eyes. Slowly, my vision cleared and I stood straight. *What should*

I do? There were so many reasons not to trust this man. As I considered my lack of options, a hysterical laugh escaped me. There wasn't anything I could do. I was at his mercy. My mouth went dry again. I licked my lips and said, "All right," but my head was screaming for me to run. Where do you run when you're under a few miles of ocean?

He nodded, his eyes burning like coals into my skin. "Good. You won't be sorry, I promise." He sure was full of himself. If there were any other choice, I'd have taken it.

He took my arm and led me to another door. His free hand turned the doorknob. "This was my mother's room. You can sleep here tonight, and I'll be right outside the door if you need anything."

The queen's bedroom. My head bobbed in agreement; the rest of me went numb.

He opened the door. I stepped in and looked around my new prison cell. It was much larger than I expected, with a vaulted ceiling reaching high overhead. The fresh, salty smell of the ocean permeated the air. A bed rested in the center of the room, surrounded by a moat of water. Red, yellow, and blue fish darted in and out of brightly colored coral. The bed fit into a depression in the floor so it was at the same level as the water, which lapped against the sides of the moat, creating a lulling sound. Along the wall behind the bed stood gigantic crystal vases filled with water and plants. I looked closer and saw tiny sea horses attached to each plant. Four posts, with sheer white material draped from one to the other, surrounded the bed. The pillows looked fluffy and inviting.

Exhaustion washed over me. Every bone in my body felt heavy as lead. My muscles screamed for rest. Moho said good night, and I watched him leave through a fog of drowsiness. When the door closed, I collapsed onto the bed and reached out for the escape only sleep could bring.

I was in a familiar place, looking into the water below. Something was down there, and I tried to get a closer look. A strange man stood on the beach, yelling at me, but I didn't pay any attention to him. A shape was taking form in the water and getting closer to the surface. Whatever was coming, it wasn't human. Before it reached the surface, a monstrous tentacle curled around my leg, plunging me into the water. I fought for air, gasping, but the grip on my leg was too strong. I couldn't escape.

I jolted awake, sweat dripping down my face, heart racing. My hair clung to my neck and back. There was no way to know how long I'd slept. The room didn't have windows or clocks. My stomach rumbled. I hadn't eaten since yesterday, or at least I thought it was yesterday.

Slowly, I eased out of bed and dragged myself to the bathroom. It was like I'd stepped into a fantasy from *Lifestyles of the Rich and Famous*. Pearls covered the walls and lined a huge clam-shaped tub in the center of the room. The shower was a cavern, tiled in polished abalone shell. A sink made of glass stood against the wall, filled with tiny fish swimming up and down the pedestal. Plumeria filled the air, reminding me of Lanai.

I sighed with pleasure and indulged myself with a hot shower. Water pounded my back, soothing tension and stress out of my muscles. I stretched my hands up on the glassy wall and let warmth wash over me. My thoughts drifted. What was it with these dreams I was having? Did they mean anything? Everything was happening so fast. This whole queen thing was really messed up. Rachel was going to love this story; her little sis, destined to be a queen. And what about this business of a Creator having a plan for me? How could my life have been anyone's plan? More important, how could a whole civilization exist without being noticed? My vision started going black again, and the pulsing dots returned. I reached up, turned off the water, and sat on the floor so I wouldn't pass out. Shivering, wet, and sitting alone on a shower floor—not really queenly behavior, was it?

Tears ran down my cheeks. My heart ached. Rachel must be so worried. Leaving her hanging, without knowing what had happened to me, wasn't fair. Even though our relationship was strained, she deserved better from me. Rachel had tried her best to make up for the loss of our parents. There was so much I needed to say to her. I so needed to get out of there. Moho had set a condition for taking me back home. I'd let him take me on a tour of the city, and the minute it was over, I'd make him take me home. I steeled myself, got up, and reached for a towel.

After putting on my now-favorite yellow pants and shirt and towel-drying my hair, I stepped out into the sitting room to find Moho ready with breakfast laid out on the table. He was grinning like a cat who'd swallowed a mouse. The sweet aroma of tea wafted over to me. My nostrils flared. Jasmine. Tea, especially jasmine tea, was my favorite morning staple. How did he know? I stopped, hands on hips, and looked him in the eye. "I don't know what you're up to, bringing out my favorite tea and all, but after I get a look at this city of yours, I still want to go home. My sister will be worried about me."

He poured a cup and handed it to me. "If it'll make you feel better, I'll send someone to let her know you are safe while we tour the city."

My hands wrapped around the warmth of the cup. The scent of jasmine reminded me of quiet mornings at home with my sis. I briefly closed my eyes and took a sip. The warmth flowed across my tongue, down my throat, and curled around my belly. Heaven.

Moho watched me intently. He patted the cushion next to him. "Come, eat, you'll feel better."

I let out a sigh and sat down. As I stuffed food into my face, I tried to imagine what Rachel would do if she were in my situation. Rachel always said to watch what people did, not what they said. Moho's smiles and empty words couldn't replace the reality that my freedom was being held hostage. Isn't that how deception usually starts—with a promise of something better?

Moho turned to me and placed his hand on my leg. "Tessa, why do you think you've been having dreams?"

"Huh?" I gasped, my mouth hanging open mid-bite. He thought it was okay to touch me like he owned me?

He squeezed my leg.

I knocked his hand away, giving him my best keep-your-mitts-to-yourself glare.

He had the sense to look sorry. "You've been having dreams about me, about our world here. You're connected to us whether you like it or not. The dreams are proof you're destined to be our queen. The Creator always sends the new queen messages through dreams." All the muscles in his body tensed as if he were ready to pounce.

Words caught in my throat, I set down my food. "How . . . do . . . you . . . know about my dreams?" Chills ran down my spine.

He paused and looked at me thoughtfully. "Because when you dream, so do I. Our dreams are connected." His hand slid toward my thigh again. I leaned away and shoved it back at him.

"This is crazy. You are crazy. Whatever drugs you're doing, leave me out of it. I want nothing to do with you or this place." I stood up. A scream built in my throat, with nowhere to go. Who would hear—and if anyone did, who would care? For the first time ever, I had only myself to depend upon. My legs shook, threatening to give way.

Moho didn't move. His eyes locked on me with unwavering intensity. "Have you ever been in love?"

I rolled my eyes. *Could this get weirder?* "No," I said flatly. "I've never met anyone I wanted to spend that much time with, and that includes you."

He put his hand over his heart and gave me a wounded look. "It's said by our people that we dream of the one person who is the partner, our perfect match. You are mine. I've been waiting for you, dreaming of you. You must be feeling those same emotions when you are near me."

I threw my hands up in frustration. "You've got to be kidding me. The only emotion I'm feeling right now is anger at you because you won't take me home. I don't believe in destiny or any of that other stuff. This Creator you keep mentioning? Never met him, but have to wonder if he's okay with kidnapping and holding someone against her will. Huh? Tell me, what does he have to say about that?"

His eyes flared. He got up, took my face in his hands, and lowered his lips to mine, his kiss hard and intense. His grip on my face was too tight, and I pounded my fists against his chest. As soon as he lifted his face, I slapped him and stepped out of his reach. He looked at me, eyes smoldering.

My lips stung. I wiped the back of my hand across my mouth. "Back off, Moho. I don't believe in any of the craziness you're spewing, so just back off. I said I would check out your city, but if you try something like that again, I'll . . . I'll refuse to go anywhere but back the way we came in!" Not that I could actually enforce that threat. My stomach churned, all the food I'd eaten threatened to come back up.

His jaw clenched. "I will show you my city. You will change your mind, Tessa. But if it makes you feel better, I won't try to kiss you again—until you're ready."

Like that day would ever come. I let out my breath. "Fine, but at least answer some of my questions."

He raised an eyebrow. "What do you want to know?"

I looked at his chest. "For starters, what is that on your chest? What does it say?"

His eyes followed my gaze. "It's a birthmark." He sighed. "As I told you, each son born to the queen is given a special gift. This birthmark is part of my gift and the reason for my name. Ka moho-alii means ruler of the sharks. Controlling the sharks of the ocean is my gift. I also have some ability to influence others."

Puna's story flashed in my head, and I shuddered.

Moho continued, "The queen's been given control over the entire sea by our Creator, to care for and manage, so controlling just the sharks is not such a big deal." He shrugged.

I tilted my head. "Not a big deal? Do all the men here have special powers?"

He crossed his arms. "No, but we can all breathe both air and sea, and we can communicate with the creatures of the ocean. Our Creator has given us responsibility for caring for the ocean and all who live in it. It's a sacred responsibility."

I shook my head. Was there any way to reach this guy, get him to listen to reason? "How in the world could someone who's not able to breathe under water ever become a queen here?"

He touched my shoulder gently. "Everyone has special gifts, Tessa. Don't underestimate your own worth. You were created especially for this, and you are the chosen queen. You are very special. You will be my queen."

Special was not how I felt at the moment. I bit my lip.

His face softened, and he pointed behind him. "Follow me."

My shoulders drooped as I trudged after him down a long hallway. At the end of the hallway an enclosed staircase wound down to a landing. My legs trembled with tension each step I took down the stairs. The sound of running water rose from below. What was waiting for me down there? At the bottom I hesitated, swallowed back my apprehension, and stepped out into an expansive room.

My jaw dropped. There were no walls. The whole side of the house was open, and I could see out over the entire city. The air was as still as the eye of a hurricane and warm enough to keep away my chills, like a womb cradling me in its embrace. Lava rock circled the city. Above, swirls of blue ocean moved across the ceiling. It was like standing under an aquarium, only this was the real thing. Fish swam by, oblivious to the city below. The sweet, musty smell of the tunnel filled the air.

Moho's home was built on the side of a cliff, very strategic for seeing everything going on below. I walked to the edge and peered over. A waterfall thundered out from under the house and fell to a pool far below. Pools of water were scattered throughout the city. Small homes and shops stood around each pool, carved right out of the rock. No two were exactly the same, each with unique patterns and carvings illuminated from within like bright candles.

Moho came up beside me, his face beaming. "Do you like it?"

I paused, gathering my thoughts. "It's like something out of a fairy tale," I whispered. Something inside me shifted. Standing there, looking out over the city, it hit me that my life could never be the same again. There would be no going back to the way things were before.

A sense of peace warmed me from down deep in my soul. Ever since the death of my parents I'd been fighting the course my life was taking, but now, it felt like I'd arrived.

CHAPTER 3

'IMI Ā LO'A
TO DISCOVER

Someone called out Moho's name, and we both turned from looking out over the underwater city to see a petite woman about Rachel's age, with long black hair, approaching Moho. Her eyes were red and swollen. She stopped just out of his reach and cast a wary glance toward me before returning her gaze to him.

Moho put one hand on my shoulder and extended the other toward this slender, exotic woman. "Akalei, I have someone for you to meet. This is Tessa."

Akalei looked up at me from under long dark lashes. "Welcome to Moku-ola, Tessa." Her voice was soft, gentle.

I shrugged out from under Moho's hand. "Thanks," I said, inching closer to her.

Moho turned his head and looked at me, eyebrow raised. He glanced at the space between us before raising his chin toward me. "This is Kele's wife."

Waves of grief poured off her like water rushing to the shore. Muscles in my chest tightened, as though each one remembered the sting grief brought with it. My hand went instinctively to cover my heart as if I could somehow protect myself from remembering the pain.

Moho stiffened. With a voice cold as ice, he turned back to her and said, "I have nothing new to report."

Akalei looked down and wrung her hands, trembling. "Moho, is there not a way we can all live together in peace?"

He snorted. "It's too late for that, Akalei, far too late."

Tears rolled down her cheeks. Without another word she turned and walked away. My eyes followed her as she left, memorizing her path so I could find her later. It took every ounce of self-control I had to stop myself from running after her, heart pounding. Maybe she could help me escape.

Moho took my arm and led me to another set of stairs. These took us straight down the side of the cliff. Each step had been carved out of the volcanic rock of the cliff, rough and hard on my feet. Vertigo kept me pressed to the wall, clutching rocks that jutted out. Even though the steps were wide enough for two, I stayed behind Moho. Every few steps, he looked back at me to check on my progress. The pounding rush of the waterfall made it difficult to hear anything. Spray from the falling water sprinkled my arms and dampened my hair. The stairs ended next to the pool, and I stepped off the last one with a sigh of relief.

I turned in a circle to take in the whole view. As I turned, I saw what hadn't been visible from above. Against the cliff wall stood a platform with a bar across the top. From the bar hung a series of hooks. On each hook hung bloody remains of dolphin, squid, seals, and even a small whale, all lifeless. My knees gave way and I dropped to the ground. The stench of rotting flesh made my stomach heave, and I leaned away from the pool to vomit.

After emptying my stomach, I splashed cool water on my face.

Something in the pool caught my eye. Deep in the water a dark shape was circling, just like in my dream. I shuddered and scrambled backward.

Moho watched me, his face hard as stone.

I wiped my mouth on the back of my hand. "What's down there?"

A smile spread across his face. "A shark. They guard all the entrances for me."

I motioned with one hand toward the hooks, not wanting to look back. "What happened there?"

His eyes never wavered but stayed focused on me. "Casualties. Sharks are hunting for Kupua, but we never know what form he'll take. We leave them hanging there as a warning to those who might want to help him."

Nausea rolled through my stomach, threatening another bout of retching. Blood rushed to my head as I doubled over and wrapped my arms around my middle. Whatever Moho's motives might be, I didn't believe he was just trying to find his mother. Brutality wasn't born from love; it came from somewhere much darker.

I had to get out of here. Every piece of information he gave brought me closer to a plan of escape. "How deep is that pool?"

He leaned over and looked into it, brushing my shoulder. "It has no bottom. It feeds out into the ocean. This is our most sacred pool, where our worship to the Creator is held."

Sacred? Nothing about what hung over the pool seemed sacred to me. Moho put his hand under my arm and lifted me to my feet. My skin crawled. He steadied me as I got my balance. Bile surged up my throat, but I swallowed it back.

"This way," he said, and he directed me down a path away from the pool.

Once we got away from the sacred pool, the air was as fresh and sweet as the open ocean. I gulped it in, trying to cleanse the smell of death from my senses. The streets were paved with polished mother-of-pearl. Reaching down, I ran my hand over the smooth surface, admiring its beauty. Pools of water lay everywhere. Beside each pool stood a home carved from polished volcanic rock and decorated with ornate symbols. The sound of the ocean moving across the ceiling provided a calming symphony in the background, reminding me of when I was a little girl and put my ear up to a large conch shell. I closed my eyes and listened, my body slightly rocking as my spirit settled. There was peace here, when I shut Moho out. It was here, wrapping around my soul.

Moho nudged my arm, breaking through the peaceful cocoon enveloping me. He motioned for me to keep walking. Peace released its hold on me as I fell into step next to him, tightness returning to my chest. There was so much I needed to know about the city if I was going to find a way out. I leaned over one of the pools and looked back at him. "Why are there so many pools of water here, what are they for?"

He leaned against the edge and crossed his arms. "Each home has a pool to allow the family a private way to enter and exit the city. Other pools are what you might know as tide pools. We don't have trees or grass, but we do have pools filled with life to explore and play with." He reached into the pool and pulled out a large orange starfish. He held it out to me, and I ran my fingers across its rough skin before he put it back and dried his hand on his shirt.

I looked around us. The streets were deserted. My throat tightened. "Where are all the people?"

He stiffened, his voice sharp. "Hiding in their homes. None of them want to face what happened to my mother. They are afraid of Kupua. Until he is caught, no one will feel safe."

I shuddered and bit back my words. I'd seen the result of his anger hanging from those hooks. I needed a safer topic.

"What about the children, do they go to school here?"

His features relaxed, and he rubbed his hand across his chin. "Yes, there are schools here, but the classrooms are not indoors. Much of what children learn takes place out in the ocean, by their experiences. We also teach them about life above the sea. They learn to read, and each one will be taken to the surface to be educated about your people. Many Hawaiians have met the children here without realizing the truth about where they came from. We are very good at blending in when we want to."

I turned toward him. "I can't imagine what our world must seem like to them. Do any of your people ever decide to stay and live above the surface?"

He shrugged. "It happens from time to time, but the draw of the sea is powerful, and it's hard to leave such a peaceful life."

I cocked my head. "Peaceful? You've spent the last twenty-four hours telling me about all the danger your family has faced, so it's not all that peaceful. Your mother and best friend have been kidnapped. And most importantly, there's so much danger here, I can't even go home."

His face turned red, and the veins on his neck bulged, throbbing against his skin. "The threat of Kupua will not be around for long. It's time we headed back." He turned and stormed back toward the sacred pool.

Visions of dead bodies whipped through my mind. Stomach churning, I held my breath and hoped I could get back without another retching episode. If only this were a nightmare and I could wake up.

CHAPTER 4

PAKELE
ESCAPE

Several men gathered on the main floor of the house, all wearing loose-fitting green pants with no shirts, just like the guards from the day before. Moisture glistened on their skin, and the musty smell of the tunnel overpowered my senses. When Moho approached, voices stilled and heads bowed. Pulling me along beside him, he walked me to the center of the room. Each man fell to one knee. Standing in the middle of the group, his face hard and fierce, Moho commanded them to rise. They lifted their heads and stood, waiting for him to speak. He gave instructions to each about protecting the city. I glanced around the room and spotted Akalei watching from the stairway. My eye caught hers, and she jumped back out of sight.

My heart raced. I whispered to Moho that I was tired and wanted to go up to bed. He waved his hand at me to go and kept talking to the men.

This was the opportunity I'd been waiting for. Once out of sight, I ran to the top of the stairs. Goose bumps broke out on my arms. Looking both ways, I caught sight of Akalei just as she disappeared through a door at the end of a long hallway. Turtle shells lined the walls, inlaid into elaborate designs patterned to mimic the movement of water. I rushed in after Akalei and caught her kneeling over a pool, handing a pouch to a sea turtle, who snapped it from her hands. She jumped up, blocking my view of the turtle.

Falling back on my heels, I blurted out. "I'm sorry. I was hoping I could talk to you alone."

Her shoulders relaxed and she sat down, the sea turtle gone. A soft purple halter dress flared out around her on the floor where she sat. Her eyes were no longer red and swollen; they were clear, green, and sparkling with interest.

I walked over and sat down beside her, my mind spinning with a flurry of questions. She smelled of plumeria flowers. I licked my lips and swallowed. "I'm sorry about Kele. You must be so worried."

She looked down at her hands. Her long, silky black hair fell around her arms, covering her like a blanket. "This is a dangerous time for all of us."

Boy, was that an understatement. I nodded and folded my hands in my lap. "How long have you and Kele been together?"

She cleared her throat. "Kele, Moho, and his brother have been my friends longer than I can remember. We grew up together, swimming in the sea, going on adventures. As we got older, Kele and I became more and more attached. I can't imagine going through life without him. We married last year. Marriage brought us together in a way words can't describe. Our people say it's how our Creator feels about us. I'm not sure I could survive if anything were to happen to my husband." She laid her hand on my arm. "I hope you find that same joy with someone as well someday."

I squirmed under her touch. Most of the married people I knew would describe it differently. "Maybe . . . I'm not sure . . . It's different on the surface. People are impatient. They hook up too fast and get in over their heads, giving away their heart before they realize the guy is a loser, or just plain mean. Some guys act like they own you, like you're property. Most are too busy to worry about what God thinks. I'm not even sure he exists."

Her eyes widened. "I can't imagine such sadness. Why do your people tolerate such things? Don't they know the Creator loves them?"

I winced. "If God cares so much, why did he take away my parents?" No one had ever been able to explain that to me.

She pulled her hand back into her lap. "I'm sorry about your parents, Tessa. That must have been tough."

I sighed. "Yeah, real tough." I paused and rubbed my eyes. Talking about personal stuff wasn't something I was used to. "To be honest, I haven't spent much time thinking about what I believe. Things have just been kinda . . . happening to me. When you're living up there, it all seems normal. Pretty messed up, I guess." Why hadn't I thought about these things? Maybe I'd taken too much for granted about my life. What did I believe in? I pulled my legs up and rested my chin on my knees. I'd kept distant from the guys who'd wanted to date me; from most of my friends too, never wanting to get too close to anyone. Loneliness haunted me, lurking in the shadows of my heart.

Akalei's voice softened. "Not messed up, maybe just confused."

My throat tightened. "Yeah." I closed my eyes for just a minute. Which world would I want to live in if I had the choice? Where did I fit?

I lowered my knees, lifted my head, and looked Akalei in the eyes. "Akalei, I need your help."

Her body tensed and her eyes narrowed.

My chin lifted a little higher. "My sister must be going crazy with worry about me. You can understand that, can't you? I have to get home, but Moho won't take me. Please, will you take me?" I held my breath.

She moved to her knees and leaned closer, green eyes alert and focused, cheeks flushed. "You want me to take you up to the surface?"

"Yes." I let out the breath I was holding. There was nothing I wanted as badly as getting back to Lanai. Every muscle strung tight, waiting for her answer. She was my only hope.

Joy lit up her face. She giggled, covering her mouth with her hand. I cocked my head and frowned at her. "Why is this funny?"

She grasped my hands in hers. "Of course I'll take you to the surface, Tessa, but first you must tell me why you don't want to wait for Moho to take you."

For a split second I considered how much to tell her, not sure how she might react. In the end I knew she deserved my honest response. It wasn't fair to deceive someone who was taking a risk to help me. She'd have to face Moho's anger—and I'd seen the reality of what he was capable of doing. I sat up straighter. "Not to be rude, but I'm feeling trapped. Moho brought me here against my will, and now he won't take me home. He says it's too dangerous, but I don't believe him. I don't think he'll ever take me back. Please, I need to see my sister and let her know I'm safe. *Please* help me." I released her hand, every nerve in my body humming.

Akalei threw her arms around me and squeezed. For such a small, delicate thing, she was strong. "Tessa, you're very perceptive, and I'm honored you trusted me with your feelings. It would be my pleasure to help you escape Moho."

I squeezed her back. Words failed me. No words sufficiently captured how grateful I was for her help.

Luckily, she didn't need me to say anything. Akalei had a plan. It was a simple plan, but I hung on every word as she explained it to me.

Later, while lying in bed, staring at fish in the moat, I played our conversation over in my head. Why was Akalei willing to defy Moho?

It was a pretty good bet it wasn't due to any loyalty to me, since she'd just met me. She said she'd grown up with Moho and his brother, and they'd been friends all her life.

I grabbed my head, realizing what I'd missed. *Moho had a brother! Where was he? Who was he? Why hadn't Moho spoken of his brother? Why hadn't I met him? What part did he play in all this?*

After I tossed and turned for who knows how long, my mind finally shifted to thoughts of Lanai and my sister. The warmth of the sun, the breeze blowing in through the window of Rachel's home, smelling of plumeria, freesia, and a host of other flowers I still didn't know the names of. Life slowed down on Lanai. No deadlines or appointments. Everything just happened so easily, naturally. It was only a ten-minute walk from Rachel's house to the market owned by Mike's family in downtown Lanai City. Downtown, a place with one gas station and no traffic lights. Everyone so warm and welcoming. Mike's family had immediately accepted me as one of their own, and he'd taken to calling me Kika. Clearly, he enjoyed tormenting me. Mike said it was because he'd always wanted a little sister. The memories brought tears to my eyes. Rachel was my rock. It was hard not having her to talk to. She'd taken on so much responsibility without my even noticing.

Someone knocked. *That must be Akalei.* I bounded out of bed and threw open the door. Moho stood there, a glint in his eye. I froze, heart leaping into my throat.

He stepped closer and put an arm around my waist, crushing me against him. He whispered in my ear, "I came to say good-bye." His breath tickled my neck. His lips brushed my cheek, and he shivered.

I forced back a gag and pushed against his chest. "Good-bye?"

He didn't flinch but kept me tight against him. "One of my sharks brought back a tip about where Kupua's hiding. We're going to find him. I'll be back in just a few hours, and then this will be over and

I'll take you home." He slowly released his grip, his hand lingering on my waist.

I stepped back away from his touch, head down, avoiding his gaze. "Good. I'm ready to go home."

He grunted, turned, and walked away.

I closed the door and slumped back onto the bed, wondering if I was wrong about him. Maybe he was trying to keep me safe. Was it possible he was telling the truth and did intend to take me home? I held my head. Was I going crazy?

Akalei slipped silently into the room, finger over her mouth signaling quiet. She wore a short black wet suit, hair braided down her back. She handed me a similar suit, and I quickly changed. We tiptoed out the door and headed to the private entrance. The guards were gone. We each placed a hand on the door, and the lock clicked and opened. Excitement pulsed through my body as I hopped from one foot to the other. It no longer mattered if Moho was being honest or not. Finally, I was going home.

Akalei grabbed my hand, and we took off through the tunnel, kicking up sand. She exploded with power. She was fast, and I worked to keep up with her, adrenaline fueling my pace.

When we reached the water, I pulled back, catching my breath. Memories of being pushed through the ocean by Moho tightened my chest.

Akalei turned and squeezed my hand. "Tessa, you'll be able to breathe as long as we're touching. I promise you'll be safe. Just don't let go of me." A spark of humor twinkled in her eyes.

My lips trembled. "Don't worry, I enjoy breathing. You may be sorry when I start clutching at you. There could be broken bones."

She laughed and pulled me over to the edge. It was time to take the plunge.

I inhaled deeply, and we both stepped off the gravel ledge into the water just inches below. Warmth enveloped me. Peace wrapped around my soul once again as Akalei pulled me deeper. This time I knew I was safe, knew what to expect. The urge to hold my breath fought with my awareness that as long as I held her hand, I would be able to breathe. Akalei raised an eyebrow at me, and I gave her the thumbs-up signal.

Akalei wore a glowing wristband that lit our way. Black sea took form under the cone of light. Fish emerged where before there were none. She pulled me up through the crack. In minutes the ocean grew brighter ahead, shining like a beacon of hope. Once out in the open sea, we were surrounded by life. Teeming schools of fish darted around us like cars swerving in traffic. Crackling sounds filled my ears. Behind us, a sea turtle followed.

I squeezed Akalei's hand to get her attention. She turned, her smile transforming into a look of surprise.

Something tugged on my leg and jerked me deeper. I kicked, trying to break free. Looking down, I saw a monstrous octopus wrapped around my leg, tentacles locked on and squeezing. Pulsing suction cups pulled my skin in a hundred different directions, every inch of my body shuddering in revulsion. Frantically, I clutched at Akalei's arm, but the octopus ripped me out of her grasp. She reached for one of the tentacles, but it shoved her backward in the water, almost like it was wagging a finger at her. I caught a glimpse of her shaking her head before I was whipped around to face another direction.

Water churned around me as my arms flailed, desperately reaching for something to grab onto. Another tentacle wrapped around my waist, pulling me deeper. Time stood still. Clouds of black ink filled the water and everything went dark.

CHAPTER 5

KUPUA

Consciousness returned slowly, bringing with it the awareness of a throbbing head. Carefully, I opened my eyes just enough to figure out where I was. Dim light filtered in. A hand laid a cool cloth against my forehead, and someone whispered, "Everything's fine, Tessa. You're safe."

That did it. Headache forgotten, I scooted up on the pillow, heat rising in my face, and growled, "I'm really tired of people telling me I'm safe when clearly I'm not."

A muffled laugh came from behind me, and I turned toward the sound, shooting arrows with my eyes.

On the bed next to me sat a guy who stopped all those arrows in midflight, his eyes warm brown circles filled with concern. Shaggy black hair framed his face, falling into his eyes, softening his features. He wasn't wearing a shirt. A scar ran along his neck and chest in a half-moon shape, standing out against his golden-brown skin. Warm tingles spread out from my stomach.

"Where am I? What happened to Akalei? Is she okay?"

He gently stuffed a pillow behind my head. The fresh smell of seawater rolled off him. "You're in a hidden cave. Akalei's fine, she's here

41

with us. I'm so sorry you had to go through this, Tessa. I'm so sorry I scared you."

I frowned. "What do you mean, scared me? Who are you? How did I get here? Why am I here?"

A smile played at one side of his mouth, revealing an adorable dimple. "Do you always ask so many questions?" His eyes twinkled. I couldn't decide whether I wanted to slap him or throw myself at his feet.

I lifted my chin. "I do when things keep happening to me I have no control over."

He met my eyes, my heart pounded a little harder, and my hands felt clammy. The tingling inside me grew stronger. What was my problem? I never reacted to guys like this.

His brows drew together. "My name is Kupua. Akalei is my friend. She brought you to me so we could talk."

Blood drained from my face, and stabbing pain shot through my head. My mind warred against the tingling warmth spreading through my stomach. Pointing my finger at him, I cried out. "You're the octopus, you're the crocodile trying to kidnap me."

He winced but didn't move from the bed.

Scrambling over the covers, holding my head with one hand, I lunged for the door. No way did I want to go through this again. I'd had enough of men from the sea. Before I could grab hold of the handle, a woman opened the door and came in. I stumbled backward. She stood tall and straight, dark eyes slicing through me like a knife through butter. Pearls weaved through the braid in her hair and wrapped around her head like a crown. She wore a long gown of dark green, belted with a string of cowry shells. Age showed on her face as tiny lines around her eyes. Dimples, just like Kupua's, graced her cheeks. She looked at Kupua, then back at me.

"Tessa," she said in a voice that commanded attention, "sit back down, and I'll explain everything to you."

Without thinking, I sat on the edge of the bed. The throbbing in my head eased.

She looked at Kupua. "Leave us alone for now."

Kupua looked at me, sadness set deep in his eyes. He stood up slowly and left the room, closing the door behind him.

He wasn't what I'd expected at all, not after everything Moho had told me. He didn't seem like a kidnapper. Of course, I only knew one kidnapper, so what did I know?

The woman sat on the bed beside me. Her features softened, and her voice lowered. "I am Queen Hiiaka, and that was my eldest son, Kupua."

My jaw dropped. Her son? Moho's brother? I was so going to kick Moho if I ever saw him again.

She shook her head back and forth. "I'm sorry you've been deceived by my youngest son. I'm going to set all that straight right now."

I didn't say a word, just sat there transfixed. The queen was clearly a woman who didn't beat around the bush.

She sat a little straighter. "I'm going to tell you the story from the beginning so you can understand everything clearly. Can you be patient and listen?"

I nodded my head. I wanted the whole story. I deserved the whole story.

She spoke softly but firmly. "Kupua and Moho were close growing up. Kupua, the eldest, knew his gift from birth. He trained for how to handle changing form and proved very good at controlling his abilities. Moho didn't know what gift he'd been given until a few years ago. One afternoon, the boys and several of their friends were hunting for pearls in unexplored caves. Moho took this search very seriously. He wanted to demonstrate to Kupua he could be just as smart and fast as their friends. While Kupua and Kele were joking around and not paying attention, Moho discovered a very large black pearl. He was thrilled and didn't hesitate to show off his new treasure. At this point, a friend, Kimo, who loved to tease Moho, grabbed the pearl from him and raced from the cave. Kimo taunted Moho, telling him he claimed the pearl for himself and planned to give it to his mother as a gift. Anger overcame Moho, and he chased after Kimo. This anger must have triggered something within him, because sharks in the area responded to his rage. Sharks circled Kimo. Unfortunately, Moho hadn't learned to master his gift and was unable to control the situation."

My hand went to my throat as I imagined how scared he must have been. I leaned toward the queen, on edge as she continued her story.

"Sharks attacked Kimo. By the time Kupua reached him, the sharks were in a frenzy, ripping Kimo apart. Kupua changed and did his best to defend Kimo, but there were too many sharks and too much damage had already been done. That's how he got the scar on his neck and chest. Kimo was killed. Moho was so shocked by what happened, he swam deep into the cave and hid. Kupua called to him, but he wouldn't respond. Kupua brought Kimo's body back, and great mourning broke out in our city. We don't have illnesses like you suffer on the surface, so the death of one of our people is a rare event. Kimo was dearly loved. Kupua and Moho's relationship never recovered. Bitterness consumed Moho's heart. Kupua didn't understand why Moho never returned to face Kimo's family, to offer sympathy. Moho refused to return to the city and live with us after that day. His resentment eats at him like a poison. This is not what our Creator intended. We are to confess our mistakes and ask forgiveness. Moho rejected love and forgiveness. He turned his back on his family and everything we represent. If we turn away from our destiny, we become lost and twisted. This is not what I imagined would happen to my son."

Tears streaked down the queen's face, sadness brimming over in her eyes. I recognized that sadness. I'd felt it when my parents died. The loss that wedges in your heart, never leaving, changing you forever. Compassion welled up inside me for all of them, even Moho.

She wiped her face with her hand and looked into my eyes. "Now they have found a new reason to battle with one another."

I looked away. Part of me wanted to comfort her; the other part, the stronger part, wanted to tell her she was crazy and run and hide somewhere far away.

She straightened, gathering her emotions and hiding them away from view. "Moho always wanted to be like Kupua. To have what Kupua had. When the king died, both Kupua and Moho knew Kupua's queen would be revealed soon. Kupua was dreaming of you, Tessa."

My stomach rolled. My head dropped into my hands, and I couldn't respond.

She brushed a stray hair away from my face. Her fingers were warm against my clammy skin. "Moho somehow used his power to intervene, to try to take you for himself. Moho kidnapped you, not Kupua. Kupua patrolled the beach that night trying to protect you. He watched over you.

"The week before, Moho came into Moku-ola attempting to capture me, but Kupua stayed one step ahead of him. Kupua kept me hidden, here, with Kele keeping watch. He's been sick with worry about you. Kupua felt responsible for your being taken against your will. His only consolation was Akalei's being in Moku-ola, letting us know you were safe."

I remembered Akalei in the room with the sea turtle, her smile when I said I wanted to leave. It all made sense now.

The queen and I sat in silence for a few minutes. Relief at finally knowing the truth strengthened me. Moho's words and actions had never been in sync. Kupua's concern for me brought back the warm tingling in my stomach. Being a pawn in Moho's plan brought back the anger tightening my chest. What a mess. There were a few choice words I'd say to Moho if I ever saw him again.

Silence broke when Akalei entered the room, worry lines on her face. "Are you mad at me?"

I shrugged. "No. But next time, just be honest with me, okay?"

The lines eased, and a smile broke out on her face. She joined us on the bed. "You can't blame me. I'd no idea how you felt about Moho."

Before I could respond, a young man poked his head in the door and announced, "You mo' bettah?" Hearing pidgin surprised me. He'd asked, "You more better," but with a strange accent, not quite like I was used to hearing on the islands. Cropped hair accentuated his round face, which also wore a big grin. Humor glinted in his eyes.

Akalei jumped up and bounced over to him, taking his hand and giving him a kiss. She looked over her shoulder at me. "This is Kele, Tessa." Much shorter than Kupua, he was sturdily built and filled out with muscles. He wore purple pants and a shirt matching Akalei's purple dress. A belt stuffed with pouches hung around his waist. "Howzit, Tessa? You ready fo' some excellent food by my brah Kupua?"

Akalei rolled her eyes. "Forgive him, Tessa. He spent too much time above water as a child." She leaned toward me, put her hand on the side of her mouth, and whispered, "He's not very good at it, but we humor him."

Kele placed a hand over his chest and crossed his eyes at her.

For the first time in a long time, I laughed. Weight lifted off my shoulders. Akalei transformed into another person around Kele, or maybe she'd just been putting on a show for Moho. "I *am* hungry. Can you give me a minute?"

The queen got up and whisked them from the room. "We'll be there as soon as Tessa is ready."

When they closed the door, she looked at me. "Please don't hold Moho's actions against Kupua. He means you no harm."

I nodded, and she pointed to a door behind me. "There's a change of clothing for you in the bathroom if you'd like to freshen up first."

My brain was on overload and needed some time to process. I stood up and made my way into the bathroom. It was small, with walls of polished black volcanic rock. A miniature waterfall trickled down into a sink carved into the wall. Small, glowing seashells hanging from rock cast soft light into the room. Rock floors warmed my bare feet, causing me to wonder if lava flowed underneath.

A dress hung in the corner. Pale green, incredibly soft, and sleeveless. I peeled off my wetsuit and slipped the dress over my head, the fabric warming my chilled skin. It hugged my body as if it had been custom-made. I splashed water on my face and ran my fingers through my long, damp hair. My stomach rumbled, and I figured the best thing to do was eat. I was very practical; Rachel would be proud.

The queen stood waiting for me. She hesitated outside the bedroom door. "Tessa, I don't want you to feel like a prisoner here. We will take you home if you want to go. Kupua and I only wanted you to hear the truth before you returned to the surface. We both felt you deserved that." Her words radiated warmth and sincerity.

Even though I was intrigued by what I'd learned from the queen, getting back to Rachel continued to be my priority. I smoothed the front of my dress with my hands. "Thank you. I do want to go home. My family will be going crazy with worry."

She led me down the hallway into a circular room with a ring of water running along the walls. High above us, shadows from the water flickered off the ceiling. Inside the ring of water stood a table very low to the ground with pillows scattered around it. Kupua, Kele, and Akalei were already sitting around the table, talking and laughing. Plates of pineapple, coconut, and papaya covered the table, and the aroma of breadfruit cooking made my mouth water.

The queen motioned for me to sit. After saying a prayer of thanks, everyone dug into the food. Kele stuffed two kiwis at a time into his mouth. He reached over and picked something off Akalei's plate. She shook her head and kissed his cheek. A constant flow of nonverbal communication passed between them. She looked at him, and he passed her a plate of pineapple, no words needed.

Kupua glanced over at Kele. "Keep eating like that, and sharks are gonna consider you a buffet."

Kele laughed but didn't slow down his consumption of food. "I gotta protect yo' skinny little *okole*."

It seemed to me Kupua didn't really need protection. The memory of octopus tentacles clinging to my skin made me queasy.

Akalei rolled her eyes and nudged him with her shoulder. "Give it a rest, you two, or you're going to give Tessa the wrong idea." She turned to me. "Don't mind those boys, they can't help themselves. I try to keep them in line, but it's a lost cause." She gave a dramatic sigh.

Kupua snorted and plucked a pineapple off Kele's plate.

Watching them reminded me how much I missed home. How much I missed the comfort of being with people who knew you, who loved you no matter what you did or said. I choked back a lump in my throat. Time to focus on something else. "What's your plan? How are you going to take Moku-ola from Moho?"

Kupua rested his chin on his hand and looked at me. His dimples came out in full force as he smiled. "What do you think we should do?"

That was unexpected. Nobody ever asked my advice. Even so, I usually had an opinion. I sat up straighter. "You should go back to

Moku-ola and confront Moho in public. Hiding doesn't solve the problem, and everyone in the city has a right to be part of what's going on." *I'd help if I could,* I thought, but I needed to get back home.

Everyone stopped eating and watched Kupua. He smiled at his mother, a warm, affectionate, loving smile that melted my heart. He turned that smile on me, and my stomach quivered like Jell-O. "That is the exact idea my mother had before you arrived here. You are both wise."

The queen winked at me.

My cheeks warmed at his words. Something about him made me weak in the knees.

Akalei sprang from her pillow. "Before we take Tessa home and go back to Moku-ola, can we take her to Turtle Cave? Please? I would love to share our special place with her." She looked at the queen for a response.

Queen Hiiaka turned to me, her eyes soft and kind. "Only if Tessa agrees and Kupua goes as well. It's not safe to travel by yourselves right now."

Kupua shot a look at Akalei. "You just don't give up, do you?"

She stared back at him for several seconds before breaking into a giggle.

Kele grabbed Akalei's hand and chimed in. "Don't let her bother you, Braddah, let's just give in, you know she get her way all da time."

Akalei punched his arm and chirped, "That's why I love you, sweetie, you always know the right thing to say." She shot Kupua a scowl.

They all turned their attention to me, waiting for me to respond. I let out a sigh and pushed back from the table. "I guess it won't hurt to check this place out before I go home."

Akalei clapped her hands and jumped up and down. "You won't regret it, Tessa. You're going to love Turtle Cave!"

Kupua shrugged. "We can go first thing in the morning. It's too late to head out now."

The queen's statement about it not being safe bothered me. I shifted on my pillow, nerves jumping. This wasn't a situation I wanted to make worse. I didn't need any more guilt on my shoulders. They needed to know Moho's plans. I stood up. "Moho is out there right now looking for you, and he plans to kill Kupua and take the queen back to Moku-ola."

Kupua snorted. "He'll never find this place. It's well hidden and protected by our friends." He sounded so sure, but so had Moho.

Queen Hiiaka got up and put a hand on my shoulder. "Tessa, Moho is strong, but he's not stronger than I am as queen. All ocean life, except the sharks, is loyal to Kupua and me. If Moho were to come close to this place, we would be warned well in advance. We have eyes everywhere. You are now under that same protection, as long as you choose to be."

What would happen if I chose not to be? Was there anyplace I'd be safe from Moho? And if she was so strong, why did Moho have control of the city?

Kupua's voice had an edge to it. "Moho is overconfident, and his bitterness clouds his judgment. However, we won't stop you if you want to return to him or leave this place now."

I frowned at him. Did he think I wanted to be with Moho? While it was true I wanted to get home to Rachel, I had no desire to ever see Moho again. A part of me felt loyalty to Queen Hiiaka. It was important to me she and Kupua set things straight. I wanted her and Kupua to be okay; it mattered to me. I crossed my arms and lifted my head. "My concern is for the safety of all of you, not my own. It's true I want to go home to Lanai, but I still hope all of you get your home back as well."

Queen Hiiaka put her arms around me and kissed my forehead. "Dear Tessa, we are so grateful for your words of support. Thank you for telling us about Moho's plans."

Akalei, who had a knack for changing subjects, ran over to me and the queen. "It's too early to go to bed, why don't we all go play with the sea horses. We could use some fun."

Queen Hiiaka let go of me and smiled at her. "Wonderful idea, Akalei. And don't worry, Tessa, this place isn't accessible to sharks. It's hidden." She took my hand, and we all walked over to the water. It was sparkling clear, with no bottom in sight.

I touched my dress. "Shouldn't we change first?"

Queen Hiiaka stroked her gown. "No need. The clothing here is made especially for water. It dries as soon as air hits it. Hold my hand, and let me show you some of the joy we experience living here."

Joy was a stranger to me. A stranger I longed to meet again. I grabbed her hand.

Kupua held back as we stepped into the pool. Out of the corner of my eye I saw him enter the water and morph into a tiny yellow sea horse with black spots. Seconds before he changed, his face beamed, like he glowed from inside. It happened so quickly, so effortlessly, I did a double take. One minute he was human, the next, something else. Knowing he could change and seeing it were very different things.

Queen Hiiaka tugged on my hand, turning my attention back to swimming. She led us through a bright tube, into a small underwater cave filled with crevices and nooks for hiding. Hundreds of small sea horses attached themselves to just about every plant in the cave. So delicate, each was covered in different patterns and colors. A current moved through the cave, causing the plants to sway.

Slowly, sea horses began to flutter our way. Hovering motionless in the water, several wrapped tiny tails into the queen's braids as she stroked their backs. Kupua coaxed a very young purple-and-white sea horse to follow him over to me. The little guy fluttered in front of my face and stared at me. I held still, not wanting to scare him away. After a minute or two, he latched himself to a lock of hair floating across my shoulder. Being so close to this delicate creature filled my heart with love. The queen watched me intently. Our eyes met, and she leaned over and kissed my cheek. Warmth and loyalty toward her and her family bubbled up inside me. Emptiness filled with longing. It was easy for me to imagine what it would be like to belong to this world, to be part of her family.

The queen whispered the sea horse's name: "Rico." Bubbles floated from her lips as she spoke. "He hopes you'll come back and visit him."

I held out my hand, and he wrapped around my finger. Bringing him to my lips, I kissed his nose. I really did want to come back.

The queen put my hand in Akalei's, said good night, and swam back home. Kele followed close behind her, waving at Akalei. I looked around the cave for Kupua but couldn't pick him out from the crowd of sea horses gathered.

Akalei and I floated in the water, not ready to leave the sea horses just yet. I savored every moment, knowing I would cherish this experience forever.

After a while, Akalei pulled away from the sea horses and tugged on my hand. "Would you like to check out some other caves? There's so much more I want to show you. Are you okay with exploring a little?"

Danger seemed a distant enemy in this secluded spot, but I knew what lurked in the deep. I'd looked into the eyes of my enemy and seen the emptiness within. I set Rico back on one of the plants swaying next to us and swallowed. Fear would not rule my life. "Why not? This might be my only chance to see your world."

CHAPTER 6

PILIKIA
TROUBLE

Visibility was terrible. Keeping close to the rocks and sandy bottom, Akalei groped around with her hand, searching for an entrance to a special cave, one she said held a surprise. Finally, she found what she was looking for, and we slipped through a dark crevice behind a rock. Cold shot through me, shivers running down my spine. Rocks scraped my arms and legs as I squeezed through the narrow passage, holding tight to Akalei's hand. We swam deep into the cave. At the very back, Akalei nudged me against a wall. One arm across my chest and a finger up to her lips, she got my attention. Pressed against the wall, I waited.

Blue lights flashed. More flickered—red, yellow, purple. Hundreds of fish emerged from the dark, emitting electrical lights, swimming in a synchronized dance of light and motion. What a wonderful gift. I squeezed Akalei's hand in thanks. It was tempting to reach out and touch them, but Akalei kept my arms pinned. Water vibrated around them, humming with electricity. Just as suddenly as it'd begun, the cave went black.

Akalei pulled on my arm, and we swam out of the cave. Visibility still horrible, I clung to her with both hands. Hairs on the back of my neck tingled. Looking over my shoulder, I glimpsed movement behind us. Something was following us. My stomach clenched. Akalei picked up our speed. All sense of peace and safety vanished. We swam as fast as possible, keeping close to the rocks for safety.

Out of nowhere, two white-tipped sharks, each about five feet long, appeared in front of us, blocking our way. White-tips were common in Hawaiian waters, very inquisitive and aggressive. We stopped and backed up against the rocks. A flash of gray-and-white fin blurred past me. A shark rammed my shoulder, trying to separate me from Akalei. Water churned around my kicking feet. It came at me again, shoving me back, harder, against the rock. I punched it in the nose, sending it spinning. A scream rose up in my throat. The second shark moved in, hovering in front of us.

Akalei wrapped her arm around me, pulling me in tight. I'd never been this close to a shark before. Black eyes assessed me, void of emotion. Razor-sharp teeth protruded from its mouth. Distinctive white tips highlighted its dorsal and pectoral fins.

The shark turned in a circle and swam off. Muscles trembling in relief, I pulled on Akalei's arm. We had to get somewhere safe, now. Akalei held on tight and shook her head, eyes wide with fear. She pointed into murky water. Danger still lurked close by. She loosened her grip and moved in front of me, covering me with her body. Over her shoulder I caught movement and shuddered.

Shadows approached. Dark forms taking shape until every jagged tooth came into view. Tail swaying, eyes rolled back, one of the sharks slammed into Akalei and shook her back and forth in its mouth as though she were a rag doll. I jerked in the water, holding on to her with every ounce of strength left in me. Her face twisted in agony. Teeth clamped on to her hip and leg. Sounds of tearing skin coupled with bubbles whooshing in our wake as we were shoved side to side. Blood clouded the water, dark red against the gray of the shark.

I jammed my finger into the shark's eye. Soft tissue gave way under pressure and popped. It didn't loosen its grip. Akalei's head fell back against my arm, and her body dangled limp. My chest tightened with need for air, no longer protected by her touch. This couldn't be happening. Anger exploded inside me and I pulled my legs up around Akalei and kicked the shark. Sandpaper skin scraped across the bottom of my feet. Nothing seemed to stop the thing. My mind spun.

Without warning, two blurs smacked into the side of the shark, and it released its grip on Akalei. I wrapped my arms around her. Out of the darkness, a dolphin swam between Akalei and me, catching our arms across its dorsal fin. Its slippery, smooth surface sliding easily below my skin. My chest relaxed as the need for air subsided. Kupua.

I rested my head against his side, watching the trail of blood from Akalei's wounds dissipate in the current behind us. If only I could turn back time, make a different decision, make this all go away.

Within seconds, we arrived back in the lava tubes, surfacing in the safety of our hideaway. Leaping out of the water for the ledge above, Kupua burst out of dolphin form in midair, landing on his feet, his face dark and brooding. He reached down and pulled Akalei and me from the water in one swift movement.

Akalei lay on her side, limp, pale as death, her dress torn to shreds. Blood pooled around her. Her flesh was ripped open from hip to thigh. I screamed out in anguish. Shaking, sobbing, I crawled to her and laid my ear against her cold chest. Faint flutters of her heart still beating gave me hope. Kupua pushed me aside and tied cloth around her leg to stop the bleeding, hands shaking as he worked. He called out Kele's name, voice pressured with urgency. Kele and the queen came running to the pool.

Kele's face contorted in horror as he dropped to his knees beside Akalei. He gently took her hand in his and called her name, but she didn't respond. Kele pulled green bandages from one of the pouches around his waist and carefully wrapped her wounds. He inserted a small ball of seaweed into her mouth, stroking her throat and face with tenderness. Gathering her in his arms, her head against his chest, he carried her into one of the bedrooms, his expression transformed into fierce determination.

Kupua followed, a storm brewing on his face. Tendons on his neck bulged as he watched Kele place his wife on the bed, hesitant to release her from his embrace.

Tears rolled down my face. She'd lost a lot of blood. I cried out, "I'm so sorry, I never should have let her take me out there. Please forgive me for agreeing to venture so far into the ocean."

Kupua turned to me and gently placed his hand on my shoulder. "Tessa, stop. You've nothing to be sorry for, this wasn't your fault." His eyes were troubled. "I'm not mad at either of you. I am worried for your safety."

He must have been following us, watching over us. How else could he have been there to rescue us so quickly? I stood there, body shaking, wishing I could do something to help Akalei. She'd risked her life for me.

He took a step closer, wrapping an arm around me. "Tessa, she'll be okay. Kele is a skilled healer."

"No," I said, my voice trembling, "Nothing about this is okay. She did nothing to deserve this. She protected me, it should be me lying there." Emotions crashed down on me. I collapsed to my knees.

Kupua fell to his knees beside me. He held me as I sobbed, stroking my hair and rocking me.

The queen walked over and set her hand on his shoulder. "Kupua, did they get away, could they warn Moho?"

Kupua shook his head. "No, the dolphins took care of them. They won't be warning anyone."

My heart eased, instinctively responding to a basic desire for justice to a wronged friend.

The queen sighed and looked over at the bed.

Kele sat rubbing ointment all over Akalei's body. The stuff smelled awful, like dead fish rotting in the sun.

I sniffed, wiping my face on the back of my hand. "Will she be all right?"

The queen laid her hand against my cheek. "Kele's doing everything possible to help her. Time to leave them both alone to rest."

Kupua helped me to my feet. I walked over to the bed and took hold of Akalei's hand, her skin hot and damp against my cool fingers, face flushed with fever. She opened her eyes.

Kele let out a groan of relief. Akalei reached up and touched his face, her eyes brightening. "Don't worry, I'll be fine, I have a great healer."

He closed his eyes and kissed her hand. She turned her head toward us, voice weak and fragile. "Kupua. Promise me you'll still take Tessa to see Turtle Cave in the morning, please."

Kupua grunted. "You need to think about getting well now, Akalei." After a brief hesitation, he added, "But I'll promise you anything if you'll focus on healing."

She closed her eyes and turned back to Kele.

Kupua took my arm and led me out of the room. In the hallway, he stopped and looked me up and down. "Were you hurt?"

"No, I'm fine. Thanks to you. How can I thank you for saving my life?"

He put his hands on my shoulders, fingers squeezing, eyes burning into my soul. "Tessa, I am responsible for you, and it would cause me great pain if anything happened to you."

My legs wobbled like rubber. I nodded and looked at my feet. I didn't want to have a breakdown in front of Kupua.

His hands slid down my arms, warm and strong, and he took my hands in his. "I'll walk you to your room."

I nodded and walked alongside him. Being alone with him stirred a fire in my soul. It burned with yearning to draw closer to him, like a moth to flame.

He leaned in and nudged my shoulder. "You did very well today with the sea horses. You're a natural with them. I think Rico has a crush on you."

A nervous laugh escaped me. "I don't know what we would have done if you hadn't shown up."

His body relaxed. I looked at him, not sure what to say but wanting him to know I didn't hold him responsible for my current situation. "Kupua, don't feel like you have to look after me. You're not responsible for what Moho did. I'll be okay."

He looked surprised and raised his eyebrow. "Do you think I'm concerned about your safety out of a sense of obligation?"

Yes, that's exactly what I thought.

He stopped, turned toward me, and spoke very carefully. "Tessa, I'm concerned about your safety because you're important to me. Not because of Moho, because of you. I care deeply about you and want you to be happy."

Could he really have feelings for me? The queen believed he had dreams about me, that we shared a destiny. Could it be true? I looked up into his eyes. My body shook. My emotional breakdown was getting closer. How much could one person take anyway?

He opened the door to my room, his eyes burning with emotion. I remembered what Moho had said about my dreams. "Kupua, before I came here I was having strange dreams. Moho told me the dreams were about him, but that didn't seem right. What do you think?"

His lips pinched together. I'd touched a nerve. "I think you can't trust anything Moho tells you. He no longer does the will of our Creator." His voice sounded strained. "Good night, Tessa. Sleep well, because we have another adventure waiting for us tomorrow."

I said good night to him, and he closed the door behind me.

My nerves buzzed. So much had happened, might take me forever to process it all. Moku-ola hadn't even existed to me a week ago. Now, feelings of attachment pulled at my heart. Sometimes the unexpected turned out to be the exact thing you needed. I certainly couldn't have planned the events of the last few days. Yet, somehow, something good had happened; new friendships had been formed, new parts of myself discovered. I'd found courage I didn't know I possessed. Was this Creator they talked about my Creator as well? Was he a part of this new feeling? Was this his plan for me?

It would be comforting if someone greater than myself were in charge. Most of all, I just wanted Akalei to recover. Someone as brave and kind as Akalei deserved better than having her life cut short. If a Creator existed, couldn't he heal her? For once, I hoped, life would be fair . . . this one time.

CHAPTER 7

HONU
SEA TURTLE

"You're not eating enough."

Sounded like Rachel. Chewing, I looked over to Kupua, who rolled his eyes at his mother. "Give her a break, she just woke up."

The queen plopped another spoonful of poi in front of me.

I swallowed, clearing my throat. "How's Akalei this morning?"

Queen Hiiaka stopped scooping food. "She's weak, and she has a slight fever, but it's come down from last night. She just needs some time. Kele's with her. He's the best healer in Moku-ola and won't leave her side until she's fully recovered."

I turned to Kupua. "Are you sure we should go to Turtle Cave? I don't want to leave her."

Kupua sighed. "She made me promise. We *must* go. I won't break my promise to her."

Queen Hiiaka added, "There's nothing either of you can do here. Go. If there is any change, I'll send a messenger to you."

Kupua got up, turned, and extended his hand to me, raising his eyebrow with a questioning look. I took one last bite of food, got up, and went to the edge of the pool. He grasped my hand, and a shiver of warmth shot through me. "What form would you like me to take?"

My breath caught. He wanted me to choose? It was an honor, and I knew my choice was important. After pausing a moment to think, I said, "Dolphin." Dolphins are one of the few mammals that can take on sharks. Loyal to their families and smart, they were my favorite. His face beamed with an inner glow I'd noticed before when he'd changed. He stepped off the ledge, morphing into a beautiful bottle-nose dolphin as soon as he hit the water.

Easing into the water next to him, I ran my hand across his sleek back. Intelligent eyes watched my every movement. What did it feel like to change, I wondered. I'd have to ask him when he was in human form again. I climbed onto his back, slipping several times on his slick skin. Once balanced, I clung tight to his dorsal fin. He submerged, increasing speed as we moved farther into the tunnel, the press of the current against my face giving me a thrill. I heard a snap and glanced behind us. A large sea turtle followed, riding Kupua's wake.

The clarity of the water made it easy to see, especially with bright light emanating from rock walls around us. We darted from one confusing maze of tubes to another. Finally, the area opened up into an underwater garden. Plants lined the floor below us, and sea kelp stood like trees, swaying as we passed. My head flipped back and forth as I tried to take it all in. Sea turtles hung suspended, motionless near the bottom, smaller fish hovering over their shells and swooping in to clean them, like a turtle car wash. Speckled eels peeked from holes along lava walls.

The moment we broke through the surface into the underwater cave, I slid off Kupua's back. He changed into human form, stood up, and strode onto the beach, clothing intact. Sitting down on the sand, he stretched out and put his arms behind his head.

I stepped out of the water, and instantly my dress dried. Twirling, I ran my hands over the fabric in amazement.

Kupua smiled. "There's a family in Moku-ola who has a special way of making our clothing. It's a closely guarded secret."

"Wow, they'd love this back home." I sat down, wiggling my toes into the sand. The sea turtle who'd followed us to the beach crawled over to Kupua, flicking sand into the air with her flippers. "This turtle seems to really like you."

He reached out and stroked the turtle's shell. "We've been friends a long time. Her name is Ka. When she was small, I saved her from being eaten by a shark, and she's followed me around ever since."

Ka looked back and forth between us, like she was following the conversation. Sand dotted her beautifully patterned shell. She stretched out her neck and snapped at the air. I tilted my head toward her. "Can she understand what we're saying?"

Kupua met my eyes, his gaze reaching into my very soul. My stomach lurched.

"Yes, she can understand me. All sea creatures can communicate with me, although the sharks won't obey me—they're loyal to Moho. But," he said with a glint in his eye, "I don't mind, because they don't exactly leave you with a warm, fuzzy feeling." He winked, the playful smile back on his lips. "Would you like me to show you how?"

I gave a snort and rolled my eyes. "Oh, please. I would know if I could talk to animals. Believe me, it would have saved me a lot of grief if I could've kept my dog from chewing up all my new shoes."

He leaned closer. His skin smelled of seawater, fresh and clean. "It's part of who you are. Remember yesterday, how it felt to be with the sea horses? You felt something, a connection to them, maybe? The Creator gave us gifts to use so we can take care of his ocean. You have gifts too."

I frowned at him. Were there things I didn't know about myself? Did I have gifts, as he called them? For such a long time, I'd defined myself by everything I'd lost. Was I missing something? I twirled hair around my fingers, playing with it like the idea running across my mind. "So, if what you say is true, what do I do?"

He motioned for Ka to come closer, and she scooted up, throwing sand behind her. She stopped in front of us, watching Kupua.

Kupua sat up straighter, his voice deep and smooth, like melted chocolate pouring across my senses. "Focus your thoughts on Ka. Ask the Creator to allow you to feel as she does, to know her thoughts."

With him so close, it was hard keeping him out of my mind, but I did my best to focus on Ka. Contentment swam through me, like I was home. Heightened smells bombarded my senses. Mussels, clams, shrimp, each with its own distinct scent, drew my interest. A salty, fishy taste filled my mouth, and I savored it . . . yuck. Devotion to Kupua followed, so strong it overpowered all other senses. Ka owed her life to him and loved him as her king, drew strength from his protection. She trusted him completely, would die for him, knew with certainty he would give his life to protect all creatures in the sea. I pulled back and looked at Kupua, not sure how to separate what Ka experienced from my own feelings.

"What did you feel?"

I reached my hand out to Ka. She stretched her neck and nudged my fingers. "I felt safe, like I was home with someone I trust."

He smiled, those adorable dimples on display again. "You were feeling what Ka felt. She is home."

My heart swelled. Excitement heightened my senses, quickened my pulse. Could I really communicate with her? Had I really felt her experience? Was this possible? "Can she tell what I'm feeling?"

Ka twisted her neck toward Kupua, playfully snapping at his feet. He shoved his toes into the sand, where they met mine. "That's more advanced. Practice receiving more, and we can move to sending messages later."

Would there be a later? Conflicting feelings battled in my heart, burning my chest. I wanted more time to get to know this amazing guy, more time to get to know myself, to unlock the talents he believed were buried deep within me. Ka trusted Kupua. Her trust lingered in my soul, making it easier for me to trust him too. He was kind and compassionate, a stark contrast to his brother.

But what about Rachel? I looked up to find him staring at me, uncertainty in his eyes. What did he think about me? Should I tell him how I felt?

I stumbled over my words. "You know, Moho scared me. All I wanted was to get away from him, get back to my sister. He tried to convince me he was my destiny, but it didn't feel right. My gut knew something was wrong. To be honest, ever since coming to Moku-ola, I don't know whether I'm dreaming or have gone completely insane. My current vote is insane."

He placed a warm hand on my arm. His words a whisper. "How do you feel about me?"

His touch vibrated through me. Every inch of me hummed, like I was hooked up to an electrical outlet. My voice wavered. "You help me understand things about myself I never knew. But . . . I'm worried I won't live up to your expectations. I'm not a queen." I swallowed hard and looked at my feet.

He turned to face me more directly. "You worry what I think of you? You're smart, courageous, and beautiful. You're what I've been waiting for my whole life. When Moho took you, I thought we'd never have a chance to be meet. I thought I'd lost the one thing I've been longing for. Tessa, I'm so happy I've finally found you."

My heart stopped. I leaned toward him, and he pulled me into his embrace. His arms wrapped around me, powerful and strong, holding me against his chest. His heartbeat pounded in my ear. His arms were comforting, like everything would be okay now that we'd found one another. His scent filled my senses, and I relaxed against him, his skin warm against my cheek.

"Kupua, I've never felt like this before." The two brothers were so different. Moho tried to control my every move, while Kupua set me free. I totally understood why Ka felt such devotion to him; he inspired loyalty. Emotions tumbled around inside me. I still wanted to get back to Rachel, but something anchored me to this place too.

After a few moments, he released me and stood up. He held out his hand. "I want to show you something."

We said good-bye to Ka and walked hand in hand down one of the many tunnels leading back into caves. Smooth polished rock, cool on my feet, replaced the sandy shore. Shells and oysters sparkled from the walls, embedded in the rock. After several turns, we ended up in a small alcove. Kupua walked over to a tide pool and reached in, pulling out a large box crafted in the shape of an oyster. He held it out for me to take.

It sat heavy in my hand; a latch on the side shimmered. I opened it, and inside lay a strand of the most perfect black pearls I'd ever seen. I looked up at him with an eyebrow raised.

He put his hand over mine. "I've been collecting pearls ever since I was a child. This strand took almost ten years to complete. I've hidden them here, waiting to give them to you. Tessa, I saw you in my dreams when I was just a boy. You would pick up pearls and toss them at me, laughing. Moho, jealous of my connection to you, tried to steal you from me."

I ran my fingers over each pearl, memorizing the unique shape of every one as they clicked against each other. Thinking of him choosing each pearl and carefully building this strand for me tightened my throat. Had I had similar dreams but just not remembered them?

He reached down and put a finger under my chin and kissed tears from my cheek.

My voice caught. "I don't know what to say."

He took the strand and clasped it around my neck. "Wearing the necklace is the only response I need." His voice trembled.

I stood on my tiptoes and kissed him on the cheek. Pearls slid across my skin as I moved, a touching reminder of Kupua's faith in a promise given by his Creator. He had no doubts. I'd felt that same, grounded certainty in Ka. Steadfast belief in who you are and your place in the world, something I'd never experienced before coming to Moku-ola but desperately desired.

Kupua sat on one of the rocks and pulled me down next to him. "Tell me more about your life before coming here, about your childhood and family. I want to know everything."

I leaned my head against his shoulder. "My story isn't all that special. When I was little, my family was very close. My sister, Rachel, and I, we did everything together. We shared a room and stayed up late at night, planning our lives. Of course, nothing turned out like we expected. When I was thirteen, both my parents died in a car accident. It was Christmas Eve. I'll never forget the smell of pine tree and cinnamon in the house. Mom and Dad went out for some last-minute Christmas shopping. We were having so much fun trying to surprise them with gifts they weren't expecting.

"But . . . it got late, and they didn't return. A police officer came to the door and knew our names. It was so strange hearing a total stranger tell us our parents were gone. Neither of us would believe it. Rachel made them take her to the coroner's office so she could see the bodies."

Kupua squeezed my hand, and I continued. "We both lived in a daze for a while, but somehow, Rachel cared for me and finished college. She married Mike and wanted to move to Lanai, not just because it was his home, but because she wanted the two of us to have a fresh start. She wanted to go where memories didn't lurk around every corner. Coming to Lanai with Rachel and Mike seemed like a better option than being alone. Mike's a good guy."

I nudged his shoulder. "I'd give anything to see his face after watching you change. Hey, what's it like to change anyway, does it hurt?"

He shook his head. "No, it doesn't hurt. It's a gift from our Creator, so it brings only joy. When I change, happiness overwhelms me, like I'm being filled with a bright light of love. The gift helps me watch over the ocean and better understand the life I'm sworn to protect."

"Wow. What's it like to be in another form? When you change back, what happens to your clothes?"

"I'm still myself when I'm in another form, but I also experience the environment through the eyes of the animal or fish I've become. My clothing's just part of the change. It's hard to explain, but it works."

He ran his fingers through my hair. "Tessa, I need to tell you I'm sorry you had such a difficult time after your parents' death. Losing loved ones is hard. You're very special and don't ever have to feel alone again."

I lifted my head from his shoulder to look at him. "Why would God take away my parents? If I'm so special, why would he do that to me?"

He leaned in and kissed my cheek. "Tessa, I don't know why your parents died." He pulled back and looked at me, sorrow deep in his eyes. "I almost forgot, there's something else I want you to see." He stood up, took my hand and led me down another tunnel.

My face felt puffy and congested from reliving my past, but my heart was light, like a burden had lifted. "Where are we going?"

He shook his head. "I'm not gonna tell you, it's a surprise."

I sniffed. "Haven't I had enough surprises? For once, couldn't something be expected?"

He laughed and pointed in front of us. The tunnel opened up into another cavern with a deep pool in the center. Sand replaced the cool stone path. Surrounding us on all sides were hundreds of newly hatched sea turtles. I dropped to my knees to get a closer look at them. They were all in different stages of going in and out of the pool.

I picked one up and stroked its shell. Its little legs kept moving as if it were still in the sand. I kissed its nose and returned it to the sand. "They're adorable. What are they doing here?"

"Eggs hatch in total safety here. It's a sanctuary. This pool has all the food they need and no predators. When they're ready, they go into the open ocean. Ever since saving Ka, protecting sea turtles has been especially important to me."

My respect for him grew. He lived his life committed to helping others, and commitment and sacrifice are rare qualities. We sat there a long time, just watching the progress of the babies moving along the beach, in and out of the water. Lanai seemed so far away.

Kupua eased back on the sand, hands folded behind his head. I plopped down next to him on my stomach, chin resting in my hands, giving him a frown.

His brows drew together. "What's that look for? Don't you like it here?"

"I'm just wondering what it would take to reconcile you and Moho. Isn't there anything worth saving in him?"

He turned his head to stare at the ceiling of the cave. "Part of me hopes there is, but I'm not sure anymore."

"What about when you were young? Was he different then?"

"Before Kimo's death, Moho and I spent all our time together.

We didn't always get along because he was constantly trying to compete with me, but we did have some fun times, and I tried to look out for him."

I crept a little closer and put my hand on his arm.

Emotions deepened his voice. "Moho didn't share my compassion for the weaker sea animals. Maybe his heart was already turning away, I don't know. He liked to swim alongside powerful fish and mammals, and he often begged me to turn into a shark or whale. One time, I became a humpback just to stop his whining. But most of all, as boys, we loved to sneak up to the surface and spy on people playing on the beaches of Hawaii. I usually changed into some creature surface dwellers would think harmless, and Moho would pretend to be playing with me. You'd be amazed how many people walked by us without a second look." He smiled, his eyes reflecting the faraway look of someone reliving a fond memory.

"On one particular day," he continued, "we came across a group of boys who had surrounded a wounded seagull unable to fly. I changed into a pelican and followed Moho along on the beach. Moho joined the circle of boys to get a closer look at what they were doing. The boys were taunting the bird and taking turns torturing the poor creature. Moho watched but did nothing to stop them. This really ruffled my feathers, and I started flapping my wings, squawking, and nipping at the boys from behind. They all turned on me and began to throw rocks at me. I got out of the way, of course, but it distracted them long enough for the seagull to escape. When the boys began attacking me, Moho lost his temper and tackled them. I flew away to put some distance between myself and the boys, and Moho jumped back into the ocean. When we got back home, Moho argued with me about rescuing the seagull. He didn't understand why I would risk our lives to save a weak and wounded bird."

He turned his head to look at me. "Moho never embraced the mission our Creator imparted to us to protect and save the life in the sea. He still believes only the fittest should survive. That is how he justifies actions such as kidnapping you. He believes if he is strong enough to take you from me, then he is the better man."

Compassion and respect mingled with longing as I stroked his smooth cheek with my fingers. "Then I guess he'll find out he is not the better man."

He placed his hand over mine and pulled it from his face. His lips brushed my fingertips, shooting chills down my spine, igniting my soul. My face flushed with warmth.

A siren call shattered the peace.

Kupua tensed, his brows drawing together. "Mother." We both jumped up and ran back to the entrance of the cave.

Popping through the surface of the pool, a humpback whale urgently called to us. Upon spotting us on the beach, its body bowed in a graceful arch and submerged, sending ripples of water rushing up onto the sand.

Kupua turned to me. "When I change, grab onto my back, can you do that?"

I nodded, and we waded into the water. Kupua instantly became a dolphin, and I scrambled onto his back, holding on as he took off at top speed. Water pushed at my face as we careened toward home, me holding on for dear life. We were back to his mother's hiding spot within minutes.

Queen Hiiaka stood waiting, her face a mask. Her lack of expression wavered as she took in the two of us holding hands. A brief gleam of joy passed through her eyes and disappeared in a flash.

"Come, sit down with me," she said.

We followed her and sat at the table, bodies tense, waiting to hear what was most certainly bad news. Kupua kept my hand in his, a welcome comfort.

The queen looked back and forth at us. "I'm so sorry to have to call you back, but something has happened."

My thoughts immediately went to Akalei, and I braced myself, expecting the worst. My fingers tightened around Kupua's hand. He froze, still as a statue, focused on his mother with an intensity any predator would envy.

It was me the queen settled her steely gaze upon. "Moho went to the surface when he realized you were gone and couldn't be found." Another pause. "He found your sister, and he has taken her to Moku-ola against her will."

I buckled over, as my world crashed down on my shoulders. Kupua put his arms around me to steady me. Rachel was in danger, and it was my fault. I wheezed for air. The thought of Moho hurting my sister rammed through my heart.

Kupua whispered in my ear. "Don't worry, Tessa, Moho won't hurt her, not as long as he thinks he can use her to get to you."

Composure slowly returned as his words sank in. I took a few deep, calming breaths. Queen Hiiaka waited patiently, watching me.

"I have been thinking," said the queen once she saw I had myself under control. "If Moho thought Tessa was taken by Kupua against her will, that she had feelings for Moho, Rachel would no longer be needed for him to bargain with."

My stomach churned. "I'm not sure I'm that good an actor."

She shook her head. "You don't have to be. We can send a message through the sea."

I looked from her to Kupua, frowning.

He saw my confusion and explained. "I can ask Ka to spread the news that I'm upset because you rejected me and are in love with

Moho. This will quickly get to the sharks out searching for information on your location, and they'll take the message to Moho. It's a brilliant idea." He inclined his head toward his mother.

I lifted both hands in the air, grabbing their attention. "How do we know for sure Moho has her? Couldn't this be another trick? I want to go to Lanai and find out the truth before we do anything else."

I glimpsed approval in Kupua's eyes. "Kele and I will escort you to the surface. We'll find out whether Moho has your sister. If he does, we'll use Mother's plan. But first, let's check out Lanai."

I didn't know whether to cry or jump for joy. Finally, I was going home.

CHAPTER 8

'OHANA
FAMILY

"You're crazy if you think I'm gonna let you go back down there with that guy." Mike waved a hand toward Kupua, keeping his other tightly gripped around my wrist. "Rachel will kill me if anything happens to you."

I glared at him. My homecoming had been nothing like I'd imagined.

"Let go of her," Kupua growled. He stood, fists clenched, eyes locked on Mike.

Puna stepped closer to Kupua. "Back off, dude."

Kele edged himself between Puna and Kupua, waving his finger. He'd come with us reluctantly, and only after Akalei had assured him she was feeling much better. "Hey, dunna give me stink eye. You is crazy to mess with my bruddah."

This conversation was going nowhere. Rachel was missing. Mike and his brother, Puna, were crazy with worry, searching the beach when they spotted us swimming ashore. Mike grabbed me out of the water and placed himself between me and Kupua. Things went downhill from there.

I pulled my wrist out of Mike's grip. "Mike, I know where Rachel is. This is gonna sound crazy, but she's being held captive in a city below the ocean floor by a guy who controls sharks. What this guy really wants is me, and I have to go back to save her. It's the only way to keep her safe." I still couldn't believe it was true. Moho really did have Rachel.

Mike's eyes flared with fear and determination. I'd never seen him so scared. "I don't think so, *keke*. This is crazy talk—if there were a city down there, someone would have discovered it by now." He reached around Kele and shoved Kupua with his hand. "What did you do to her, did you drug her?"

In a flash, Kele turned and grabbed Kupua, pushing him back a few steps, holding on to his arms. Conflicting emotions danced across Kupua's face: frustration, anger, empathy, and worry. I watched as he took deep breaths, getting his flood of feelings under control, fists still clenched at his sides. He slowly lifted his gaze, eyes fierce, gritting words out between clenched teeth. "Listen . . . Mike, we . . . are . . . telling . . . you the truth. Why would we bring Tessa back here if we were drugging her or wanted to hurt her? I am trying to protect her. We all want Rachel back, but you are going to have to trust us."

Mike looked like a volcano had gone off inside his head, his neck and face bright red. Puna moved in front of him, grabbing his shoulders. "Mike, man, you've got to calm down and think. Losing it won't help Rachel. Let's at least listen to what they have to say."

I moved closer to Mike and put my arm around his thick shoulders. He was family, and his pain stung deep into my heart. "You know I love Rachel and would never make up a story if she was at risk. Think about it, Mike. Have I ever lied to you?"

He deflated like a popped balloon. "No, keke, you've never lied." He covered his face with his hands, visibly shaking. "I don't know what to think. First you go missing, then Rachel. Now these guys show up with a story no sane person would believe."

Kele released his hold on Kupua, who stepped forward, compassion filling his eyes. "Mike, I get this is hard to accept. In fact, your response is what my people have fostered for centuries. We don't want you to know about us or believe we exist. But I can prove we are who we say. If I go back into the ocean and fly out as a seagull, land on your shoulder, then return to the sea, will that convince you?" Exposing his secret cost him, the price evident in the pulsing veins on his neck, the tension vibrating through his muscles.

Mike and Puna stared at him as if he were from another planet. Mike took a step toward him, shrugging, with a smirk on his face. I recognized that look; he was sure Kupua was bluffing. "Okay, if this happens like you say, I'll listen to your plan."

Kupua nodded, turned, and walked into the sea, disappearing beneath the waves. Within seconds a seagull bobbed to the surface, taking flight in our direction.

I watched Mike's face as the seagull landed on his shoulder. He dropped to his knees, his expression frozen in disbelief.

Puna's mouth dropped open, and he looked at Kele. "No way."

Kele grinned and crossed his arms. "Way."

Mike let out a sigh, and the tension eased.

With a loud squawk the seagull spread its wings and lifted off Mike's shoulder to land on mine, rubbing its head against my cheek. I stroked its back with my fingers, and its feathers ruffled in pleasure before it took off back to the sea, diving below the waves.

Kupua emerged from the surf and strolled back, stopping in front of Mike. "Rachel won't be harmed by my brother as long as he believes her presence will draw Tessa back to Moku-ola. I promise you, we'll find Rachel and bring her back to you safe."

Resignation echoed in Mike's voice. "If you don't bring Rachel and Tessa back unharmed, we will hunt you down. I don't care who or what you are, we will find you." They stood there, eyes locked, for a long time.

Kele clapped his hands together. "Kay, den, we go sit down, talk nice?"

Puna put his hand on Mike's shoulder and gave him a friendly shake. "I'm ready to talk. How about you, Mike?"

Mike got to his feet. "I'm listening."

We all moved a little farther onto the beach. Shipwreck Beach was my favorite on the island. Usually quiet and empty, today was no exception. Water off this beach was too treacherous for most people to risk. The rusted hull of the World War II *Liberty Ship* loomed offshore. I smiled and tipped my face toward the sun. Wind whipped through my hair. Familiar smells of plumeria, gardenia, and ocean mixed together, comforted my senses. My world might be upside down, but I was home with family, and we had a plan.

Puna topped off my moment by retrieving a basket of food from his jeep. "How about some grub while we talk?" he shouted over his shoulder.

Kele didn't hesitate to dig in and start shoveling the food. "E'y, brah, dis is some great food!"

"I agree, Puna, this looks delicious!" I picked out my favorite, stuffed grape rolls with hummus.

Mike didn't touch the food, clearly not ready to make nice. It's hard to stay angry when you're sharing a meal, which is probably why Puna went for the food.

Kupua outlined his plan, and Mike grudgingly agreed—he didn't have a lot of choice. Pain and worry flashed across his face as he looked from me to Kupua. I kissed his cheek. "Mike, we're gonna do everything we can to get Rachel back."

"Take me with you. Rachel is my wife. I have every right to risk as much as you to get her back. There's no way I'm just gonna sit here and wait."

Kupua turned to me, his brow raised in question. I shrugged. Mike had a point: who was I to deny him a chance to help? Kupua looked over at Kele, who had his head down, concentrating on digging his feet into the sand. Kupua huffed. "You don't know what you're asking. If I take you to my world, you'll have to swear loyalty to us, agree to keep our existence a secret, even from the rest of your family." He glanced over at Puna, who had gone off to collect firewood, expecting us to stay on the beach.

Mike put a fist over his chest. "Tessa can vouch for me. My word is gold. I will keep your secret, do whatever it takes to keep Rachel and Tessa safe."

His devotion warmed me. "He's right, Mike is solid. If he says it, he'll do it." He cast a glance my way, acknowledging my words, a smile of thanks in his eyes.

Kupua stood up, casting a glance toward Kele. Kele nodded and immediately walked over to where Puna was collecting wood and knocked him over the head with a log. He dropped in one strike. Mike rose to protest, but Kupua slammed his fist in the side of his head. Mike staggered, knees buckling, then he dropped to the ground, out cold.

I jumped to my feet, stunned. Seeing Mike crumpled in the sand tightened my throat in panic. "Why'd you do that?"

Kupua shook his hand, wincing. "Wow, guy's got a hard head." He looked at me. "Tessa, Puna can't come, so we had to knock him out, and I don't want Mike to panic when we take him under or remember how to get there. He's too big a guy to control underwater if he decided to fight us. If he's coming, this is the only way."

Kele strode over and sported a big grin, picking up Mike across his shoulders. "Dat was fun, brah."

We waded into the water. Deadly currents didn't threaten much when you were diving deep on the back of a dolphin. Boy, had my life changed.

CHAPTER 9

ʻŌLELO MAKUA
A TALK WITH MOTHER

Back under the sea, alone in my room, the full weight of Kupua's plan bore down on me. Phase one was in play. Kupua had sent out the message that I'd rejected him and was pining away for Moho, was even willing to marry him. We'd also implied that Kupua was willing to negotiate with Moho for my return, and he was waiting for a response.

The queen opened my door and peeked inside. "Tessa, can I talk to you?"

I sat up and waved her in. "Sure."

She sat on the bed next to me. "There's more you need to know before facing Moho again."

I swallowed, pulling my knees tight against my chest. Somehow I knew I wasn't going to like what she was getting ready to tell me. Tension radiated through my neck and shoulders. "Give it to me straight. At this point, nothing's really gonna surprise me."

She took my hand in hers, gently squeezing. "You know how much is at stake, but you haven't yet accepted the key role you play in what's happening. Tessa, you're at a critical point in your life. The choices you make will impact everything that comes after." She wrapped her arm around me, and I leaned against her shoulder.

My body relaxed as peace washed over me. Her voice soothed my ragged nerves. She provided shelter in the midst of my storm.

She stroked my hair. "The only way to stop Moho from coming after you once and for all is to accept the authority of queen, to acknowledge the destiny our Creator has planned for you. Once you are queen, Moho will have no power over you, but if you don't, he will never give up. You don't think you can be queen, because you have only been looking behind you. It's time you started looking forward."

I squirmed under the truth of her words. She seemed so sure of what she believed. Perhaps I'd chosen the easy path. "You might be right. I think I've been waiting for my life to start. But this is all new to me, so it's kinda hard to accept. Being queen is a whole lot of responsibility. I've never been good at taking care of myself, so the thought of having to take care of the entire ocean is really overwhelming. Rachel always took care of me—she should be your queen." My shoulders relaxed as I let go of the words, as if speaking them released the worry I'd been carrying.

"Tessa, I'm sorry I don't have more time to prepare you, but you can do this, and you won't be alone."

Kupua stuck his head in the door. "Can I join you two?"

The queen looked at me. "Is it all right with you?"

He was my undoing. I nodded as tears filled my eyes. "You are crazy to think I can be queen."

Kupua's eyes softened as he entered the room. "Tessa, why do you doubt yourself? You'll be a great queen. No matter what happens, I vow I'll protect you and your sister."

Protection wasn't what I was worried about. It was changing the course of my life—well, actually, choosing a course for my life—that weighed heavy on my shoulders. They didn't have any doubts, but I had enough to cover us all. I reached up and took his hand.

"Kupua, I know you will do everything you can to keep us safe."

He knelt in front of me. "Then why are you scared?"

Why was I so scared? I bit my lip. "I don't know how I'll do this, how to live up to all your expectations. I wasn't raised to be queen. Before I came here, I had no idea what to do with my life. Now, I have to choose so quickly. And the choice I make matters a lot."

Kupua smoothed the hair away from my face, his touch soft and gentle. "If you don't want to do this, we can think of something else. I don't want you to feel forced into it. That would make us no better than Moho."

I grabbed his chin, forcing him to look into my eyes, to see the truth there. "No, I will step up and do this, I will be queen, but that doesn't mean I don't have fears. Kupua, you've got to understand, things are happening so fast."

"You don't have to do this alone. Tessa, we'll all be with you. We'll all help you with this responsibility. Let me share the burden with you."

My heart pounded so hard, I felt it in my throat. Kupua was everything I wanted but had never expected. Words stuck, choking me. "Yes, I'm depending on all of you to help me. You've changed my life. Kupua, can't you also be crowned king? After all, this is your birthright, not mine. Why can't you be king?"

Hope and longing shone from his eyes briefly before he closed them, rubbing his hand at his forehead. "This has never happened before. I guess I really don't know the answer. Mother, can you tell us?"

I frowned at him. Why did he have to ask his mother? What was the big deal anyway? After all, wasn't he supposed to be king?

Queen Hiiaka looked back and forth between us, and her razor-sharp gaze landed on Kupua. "This talk is really between Tessa and me. Kupua, go check on Mike. He should be waking up soon."

His head drooping, he got up and slunk out the door. He looked back over his shoulder and winked at me right before closing his mother and me in the room together.

The queen kissed the top of my head. "Requesting Kupua to be crowned king has huge implications for your future, and you must not make this decision lightly. Tessa, if Kupua is crowned, he cannot be uncrowned. What you are asking has never been done in Moku-ola. We will have to wait on this decision."

My head fell into my hands. "Wait for what? I can't do this alone."

"You aren't alone. But the king has always been married to the queen, to rule as partners united. Give this some time. It is not a decision for today, and it is not one you have to make by yourself. Agreeing to be queen of Moku-ola is enough for one day, don't you think?"

I exhaled and lay back on the bed, exhausted from our conversation but strangely calm now that the need to make a decision no longer weighed heavy on my mind and I'd ensured Rachel's safety. Life here was so different than above the surface. Every step I took toward this new life made me more certain I didn't want to return to the life I'd known. It would be like going backward. I was ready to move forward. Confidence replaced doubt and uncertainty. Life held purpose. Whatever I faced, I wouldn't be alone.

CHAPTER 10

A'O, 'OLELO A'O
INSTRUCTION

Training. The plan for the day was to train me, build up my skills. The queen and I walked into the main room and found Kupua sitting with two large, sleek sea lions, who barked a greeting as we approached. Kupua looked up, smiling, and reached out for my hand. I joined him and asked, "What are their names?"

Queen Hiiaka placed her hand on my shoulder. "Why don't you ask them yourself?"

I shot her a scowl. She sure could be pushy when she wanted something, and she was serious about training. I grudgingly reached out and put a hand on each of their heads and focused. Strong family bonds tied them to each other. A mother-and-daughter pair. Extremely social animals, they both considered Kupua and the queen part of their family unit. It was easy to understand—they were burrowing into my heart as well. Naturally playful and curious, both sea lions hoped I liked to play as well. Exhilaration coursed through my veins as the excitement of the hunt washed over me, calling me into the sea. I patted their heads. "Nice to meet you,

Mimi and Lizzy." Wet noses nuzzled my hands, whiskers tickling my palms.

Kupua laughed, his face lighting up with joy and approval.

Queen Hiiaka patted me on the back. "You truly have a gift for this, Tessa."

Mimi and Lizzy knocked me over, covering my face in wet, slurpy kisses. Their breath reeked of fish, and I covered my face with my hands. Lizzy responded by rolling me over to the water and pushing me in. She was stronger than she looked.

When my head bobbed up and I found myself nose to nose with Lizzy, who clearly wasn't done playing, Kupua doubled over, laughing.

The queen called her off. Lizzy sulked over to her mother, and believe me, sea lions can really pour on the drama routine. She sat, head drooping and flippers over her face. I liked her.

Kele, Mike, and Akalei joined us. I jumped out of the water, dripping, as I ran to hug Akalei. She looked like her old self, bright and happy. "It's so good to see you up."

She squeezed me back. "Takes more than some nasty sharks to keep me down." Despite her brave words, her hug wasn't as strong as I remembered.

I turned to Mike. "Hey, Mike."

He pulled me into a bear hug, his face grave. "Hey, Tessa. This place is a trip."

"Yeah, but it grows on you." I pulled back and assessed how he was handling all the new developments being thrown his way. He looked weary, eyes bloodshot and hair shooting out in all directions.

He pinched the bridge of his nose, squeezing his eyes shut for a moment, fighting back strong emotions. "When do we go after Rachel?"

Queen Hiiaka cleared her throat, catching our attention. "Before we go to Moku-ola to rescue Rachel, Tessa needs preparation. Kupua and I will be taking her out into the *makai*, the open ocean. A family of dolphins has agreed to travel with us to mask our presence so we won't be detected by sharks. Moho will not leave Moku-ola now that he has Rachel to guard."

Mike's face dropped, and my heart sank with him. There had to be something we could do. "Before we leave, is there any way to make sure Rachel isn't being hurt or in immediate danger?"

Queen Hiiaka thought for a moment. "Maybe, if Rico is willing, he could sneak into Moku-ola unnoticed and check with our spies. If he agrees to go."

Confusion passed across Mike's face. "Who's Rico?"

I laid a hand on his arm. "He's a friend who happens to be a seahorse." *Wow, never thought those words would come out of my mouth.* Mike looked at me and shook his head, skepticism etched on his features.

Queen Hiiaka sent Lizzy to summon Rico to the pool. It wasn't long before they both returned. Queen Hiiaka put her feet in the water and closed her eyes. After a few minutes, she smiled and glanced back at us.

"Rico has agreed to go. He'll find out what's happened to Rachel and if she has been harmed. He's very pleased we've asked for his help." We all watched Rico swim off on his mission.

"Tessa, we don't have time to wait for him to return. We will likely be back here before Rico is. We must leave now."

Mike, Kele, and Akalei wouldn't be joining us. Instead, they would be monitoring messages coming and going out of Moku-ola. Mimi and Lizzy however, were welcome to tag along.

"Okay." Time would go faster if I kept busy. "Let's go, I'm ready."

Our odd little group of five started out for sea: Kupua as a dolphin, me holding hands with the queen, and Mimi and Lizzy darting between us. Anticipation buzzed through me like a live wire. As soon as we left the tunnels, dolphins surrounded us—almost two dozen, a large family group. As we swam along, I sensed things about them. A very cunning species who worked well together. Constant communication occurred among them, strategizing and planning their next moves like a well-honed team. Kupua and the largest male seemed to be discussing something. It took me a moment to register I was picking up on their experience without even touching them—something else I didn't know I could do. Excitement thrilled through me.

As a group, we moved closer to the surface so the dolphins could get air. Kupua swam under me, and another dolphin slid under the queen. Before I knew what was happening, I burst out of the water and flew through the air on his back. He leaped in play with the rest of the dolphins. I wrapped my arms around him and urged him to go faster. He was happy to comply, and we were quickly soaring through the air, weaving in and out of the waves at top speed. Delight filled my soul, and my laughter rang out with abandon, experiencing a moment of true escape from the worries and fears that plagued us.

It didn't take long to travel a good distance away from Moku-ola. We started to slow as we approached a small body of land that showed no sign of human life anywhere. The dolphins took us into the shallows, where we swam the remaining distance to shore. Once on the beach, Kupua changed into human form, and I hugged him.

"Thank you for that," I told him, and he squeezed me tighter. "I can't remember the last time I had that much fun—maybe never."

"It's only the beginning."

My spirit soared. Life in Moku-ola would never be boring or mundane. So many possibilities opened up to me.

We joined Queen Hiiaka under the shade of a palm tree. Mimi and Lizzy waddled over to lounge next to us. Lizzy nuzzled up to me and put a flipper around my shoulders. I reciprocated the affection by rubbing under her chin, which resulted in crazy flipper shaking. Warmth from the sun beat against my face. A soft breeze dried my hair, and I almost forgot why we were there until the queen's voice broke my bliss.

"Tessa, you have learned how to listen to individual sea life. Now it's time to move to the next step and speak to them." Insecurities ate away at me. What if I couldn't do what she asked, wasn't really as talented as she thought?

"Concentrate on Lizzy. Ask her to do something and push the thought toward her."

Sounded easy in theory. I looked at Lizzy, who was busy trying to reach an itchy spot on her back, body twisting and flipper flapping up and down. I asked her to give Kupua a kiss. With all the focus I could muster, I pushed the thought toward Lizzy and concentrated on her. She perked up and whipped her face around to look at me. Even though I was trying really hard, it still took me by surprise when she actually waddled over to Kupua and gave him a big, cold, wet smack in the face.

The queen started laughing, and I let out a big sigh of relief.

"Now try something farther away. Step into the surf and contact the dolphins."

I inhaled, pushing my doubts into the back corners of my mind. Cool water danced around my ankles as I stepped into the ocean. I chose the large male who had been communicating with Kupua earlier. Would he listen to me?

I asked him to leap out of the water. A few minutes passed. Nothing happened. I rubbed my forehead and tried again, tensing with frustration . . . still nothing. I dropped my arms to my sides and turned toward the queen.

"What am I doing wrong?"

"Just because you ask doesn't mean he'll cooperate. Did you say please?"

"Really? Dolphin etiquette?" Not even Puna would believe that one. This was killing me; it wasn't easy to stay so focused. Turning back toward the open ocean, I tried again, this time asking him to *please* jump out of the water.

Within seconds, he burst through the surface and did a flip. I gasped and looked over at Kupua. Approval, affection, and admiration shone on his face. My stomach did a flip.

"Okay, Tessa, now for the big stuff."

Big stuff? Was she crazy, what had I just been doing? My head throbbed.

Kupua interrupted her. "How about a break first? I want to show Tessa some of the island."

Queen Hiiaka narrowed her eyes at us. "All right, if you must, but don't be too long, we have a lot to do today."

Kupua extended his hand to me. "What do you say, Tessa, care to explore with me?"

"Sounds good to me." I grabbed his hand and waved at the queen, grateful for a reprieve. Within minutes of setting off at a run, we were in thick rain forest and out of view of the beach. Kupua led me to a freshwater pond surrounded by lush plants and trees. The air was sweet with the scent of tropical flowers. Cool grass cushioned my feet. Kupua dropped down and pulled me with him.

"I've been looking for a way to spend some time with you, just the two of us." He stroked my cheek with his fingers and leaned in, gently kissing my lips. As I reached up to touch his face, a blast of heat hit us as if someone had opened up the door to a furnace. My eyes stung, and my skin felt singed.

"Where did that come from?"

"Don't know," he said. "Let's go find out." He stood up, pulling me with him. We followed the wilted grass, headed in the direction the blast had originated. After walking a short distance, we came upon a small crater with a hole in the center. Bones lay scattered around the hole. I moved to look more closely, but Kupua held me back. "Wait, can you feel it?"

"Feel what?"

"The vibration. Something below us is moving." A tremor rippled through the sand below my feet. I kept my eyes on the hole. Within seconds, another blast of hot air and ash shot out, spewing small bones and fragments everywhere.

I covered my nose, gagging on the smell of sulfur. "Are we on a volcano?"

He searched around, picking up and examining bits of debris. "No, it's not a volcano. I have an idea what it might be but can't be sure. I don't think we should stay here. Let's get back to the beach.

"Wait, don't you want to know more about this?" I knew *I* was dying of curiosity.

"Tessa, I have a theory but want to find out more before I put you in danger by exploring something we don't understand." He grabbed my hand and pulled, but I resisted.

I was tired of being ordered around. "Sorry, aren't queens in training supposed to be brave? Shouldn't I decide? Isn't my taking charge what all this instruction is really about?"

His head drooped, resignation in his face. "I don't like it."

I touched his shoulder. "Let's just poke around a little, nothing extreme."

He sighed. "Okay, what do you suggest?"

"How about we start with dangling something down the hole and see if it gets burnt up."

He rolled his eyes. "You want to get close to the hole? How is that not extreme?"

I ignored him and started gathering up discarded bone fragments. I examined one closely and turned to him. "What animal do you think this is from?"

He stepped closer and his face went pale. "That's from a whale."

"A whale? How would a whale bone get here?" My curiosity was killing me. I started weaving together palm bark until I had a long, strong rope with a bone tied to the end.

Vibrations continued to rumble beneath us. Kupua helped me throw one end of the rope into the hole while I held the other end and waited. My hands grew sweaty as I tensed for something to happen. The vibration stopped. Silence. I started to inch closer, but Kupua grabbed my arm. Just as I was turning to tell him it was okay, a loud shriek rocketed out of the hole, piercing my eardrums, catching me off guard. The rope lurched and pulled me with it. I skidded along the ground. Kupua pulled back on my arm just in time to keep me from plummeting into the hole. I let go of the rope and let out my breath.

"What was that?"

He frowned. "I'm not sure. Let's go, I'll tell you my ideas when we're safe." This time I didn't argue. Even my curiosity had limits.

Back at the beach, the queen was playing in the surf with Lizzy and Mimi. Kupua didn't mention the strange crater and gave me a stern look when I started to tell her. Why wouldn't he want her to know? I glared back at him. He had some explaining to do when I got him alone.

The queen seemed unaware of anything amiss. She and Kupua took my hands and led me into the ocean. We waded out until we were about knee deep and sat down so the water was at our waists. They stretched me out so I floated next to them, water lapping against my cheeks.

Queen Hiiaka squeezed my hand. "Now listen not just to one, but to the collective communication going on in the ocean. Be still and open to what is out there."

I closed my eyes, shutting out all other thoughts. The ocean spoke to me, came alive; it was a very noisy place. Crackling filled my ears. Thousands of small shrimp called out, more like a chorus than a conversation. Information about the location of food, where they all were, and something I didn't quite understand about the temperature of the ocean.

I focused on widening my range and immediately heard the dolphins who had brought us here, but this time I really heard them. Sophisticated communication about goals, strategies, how to hunt, how to keep each other safe. They had complex relationships with each other. At the moment they were strategizing the best way to return to our hiding place without being detected. Fin, the large male, was the leader. He was incredibly intelligent and brave. We were in good hands with him, and he had a plan to keep us hidden. His mate, Bee, was also smart, but she was focused on something else. Bee was pregnant.

I pushed my mind farther out. There were so many sounds, so much going on, it was overwhelming but exhilarating at the same time. Whales talked over long distances. Schools of fish hummed. Human boats and motors, something splashing far away, and a very disturbing sound of fish in distress. I didn't want to hear their distress, but it was there. Cries for help as fish were caught in nets, panicked. I shivered. Their cries cut through my heart. The desire to rescue them consumed me. In fact, I wanted to protect all life in the ocean. The urge to respond and protect was so strong, it overpowered everything else I was feeling. This was an entirely new emotion for me. I never felt protective over anything. I kicked forward, instinctively moving toward the calls for help. Kupua grabbed my arm, holding me back.

"I'm sorry Tessa, you can't help them right now, there's too much danger out there, searching for you."

Then something snapped me out of my personal struggle. Dark, twisted thoughts approached. The single-minded focus of a killer vibrated into my awareness. My eyes shot open. A large shark headed toward us, and he was focused on me, sent on a search by Moho. Death wove through his thoughts. I sat up out of the water and yelled, "Shark!"

Kupua spun into action and had me on the beach before I could blink. Once I was safe, he dove back in the water and disappeared from sight. Fear clenched my chest. I closed my eyes, determined to use my new gift to reach out to him.

Kupua changed into an orca, a mammal that could easily take on a great white shark, and it was a great white, I was sure of it. The dolphins trailed him, and they all worked together with one goal, to kill the great white intruder.

The queen sat down beside me and wrapped her arm around me, but I stayed focused on the unfolding drama. The thought of something happening to Kupua was more than I could bear. And I was worried about Bee and her unborn baby. If anything happened to them, I wasn't sure how I'd react. My emotions now irretrievably connected to all life in the sea.

Kupua was out in front of the dolphins, but several of them had changed course and were positioning themselves behind the shark. I knew exactly when the shark became aware of them. Everything sped up. The shark and Kupua circled each other, looking for weaknesses.

The dolphins went deep to come up under the shark and strike in his most vulnerable area, the stomach. Fin struck first, and it was a good blow. The shark faltered, and Kupua wasted no time, jumping on the opportunity to attack. He ripped a chunk out of the side of the shark. The shark spun around—he was fast—and caught Kupua's tail, barely nicking the end with his teeth. A sharp stab of pain ran through me, and I cried out. Before the shark could cause any more damage, Fin came barreling up from underneath it and plowed into its stomach with such force, they both went airborne. When the shark plunged down into the water, another dolphin struck a second blow. The shark's body went limp and lifeless.

I let out a sigh of relief and opened my eyes. The queen stared at me, her eyes wide with disbelief.

I didn't understand her expression. "What?"

"You followed what was happening through their thoughts."

"Isn't that what you've been teaching me to do?"

"Yes, but you weren't in the water. No one, not even I, can track their thoughts unless I'm in the water. Tessa, this is amazing, you're gifted beyond what we imagined."

I started to respond, but Kupua dragged himself onto the beach. I ran to him. Blood oozed down his leg. The wound didn't look serious, but it would need attention soon. Luckily the shark hadn't gotten a good grip on him.

"Hurry." He took a shuddering breath. "The shark's dead, but others will follow soon with the smell of blood in the water. We have to leave now." We didn't argue. I took the queen's hand, as Kupua was too weak to carry me. He changed into a dolphin. His wound still visible, he struggled to swim. Two young female dolphins allowed the queen and me to grab hold of their dorsal fins, and we sped back to our hideaway—without encountering any more sharks.

Kele met us when we arrived and immediately wrapped Kupua's leg in green bandages.

Kupua's face contorted in pain, and I grabbed his hand.

"Will he be okay?"

Kele and Kupua grunted in unison. "Dis nothing for my brah, he be fine." Tension eased off my shoulders.

Kupua nudged me. "I told you, I'll keep you safe."

I raised my brow at him. "Looks like you might need me to keep you safe as well."

He chuckled.

Rico arrived just minutes after Kele finished bandaging up Kupua. When I saw him waiting at the edge of the pool, my heart skipped. Now that my skills were getting better, I took his report directly, putting my feet in the pool. Not that I needed to be in the water to sense his thoughts, but I couldn't resist the chance to spend time with him. He curled himself around my big toe. I concentrated. Rico had gotten his report from a crab living in the tide pools of Moku-ola, a very reliable source, Rico told me. Rachel was fine. She was very angry and shouting all sorts of things the crab didn't understand, but she was strong and healthy. Picturing Rachel releasing her fury upon Moho brought a smile to my face. That was my sister, all right. Rico went on to describe that she was being kept locked in a hidden room away from people but was being treated well otherwise. Rico believed Moho wouldn't hurt her as long as he thought there was a chance I would return to Moku-ola. Well, that meant our plan was working. I thanked Rico for his help and sent him back to his family.

I turned to find everyone watching me.

"Our plan is working." Too bad it didn't make me feel better. Every step in our plan brought me closer to being crowned queen. How could I possibly take care of an entire ocean? And what was spewing up whale bones in the middle of nowhere? Were there any more mysteries lurking about, waiting to pounce on me? Because I certainly seemed to be a magnet for all things weird.

CHAPTER 11

'ĀNELA
ANGELS

My definition of *bizarre* was being redefined daily. In fact, a month ago, I would have considered myself insane for my current definition of *routine*.

My feet dangled in the large pool of water in the dining area. Kupua was off somewhere with the queen. A few moments alone were just what I needed. Solitude was something I treasured but hadn't gotten much of since arriving in Moku-ola.

Strange sounds began vibrating in my head, louder and louder, pounding at my temples. With my eyes closed, I concentrated on identifying the source. Something was trying to communicate with me. The vibrations seemed to be coming in a pattern. I got the distinct impression I was being called. But called to what and by whom, I had no idea.

Focusing all my attention on the sound in my head, I turned inward, blocking out noise from my surrounding environment. Kupua returned and sat down next to me, bumping my shoulder. His leg had already healed under Kele's care.

"What are you doing?"

"Something is calling me, but I have no clue who it is or what it wants. So far, all I can make out is a pattern of vibrations I think are calling me to them."

Silence. I opened my eyes and looked at him. "What? What's wrong?"

"Tessa, I know who's calling you." Worry brewed in his eyes, swirling like a storm unleashed.

"Great, please tell me so I can stop driving myself crazy trying to figure it out."

His face lost all its color, and his brows wrinkled. He wrapped his arm around me and drew me closer to him. "You're being summoned."

"Summoned? By who?" This couldn't be good.

"The Anela are summoning you. They are the guardian angels watching over the ocean, messengers for the Creator. If they call you, it's to test whether you are worthy to take on the responsibility of being queen."

My body trembled uncontrollably. I didn't think I could take any more tests.

"What exactly do you mean, test me?"

The vibrations got stronger, pulling at me, tearing my brain apart from the inside. I tried hard to shut down my mind, but nothing seemed to work.

"You cannot resist them. Don't try, it will only cause you pain. We must go to them. There's no escape once they have called."

He hadn't answered my question. My head pounded. He stood up and pulled me to him. My hands covered my ears in a feeble attempt to block out the vibrations.

"Tessa, listen to me. I must take you to the Anela right now. We have no choice. You cannot run from the Creator."

"There's always a choice, Kupua. I won't go. I'm not ready." I stepped away from the water, determined to put some distance between me and the annoying Anela. Pain exploded across my temples, bringing me to my knees, hands grasping my head as if I could block out the intruders.

Kupua whispered in my ear. "There's no way to prepare for the Anela. They don't test you in the way you think. They test your character, the very essence of who you are. Please, if you don't answer the call, they will not stop. Everyone destined to rule the ocean is tested. I know because I've been through this, Tessa. I'm sorry, but we must go. You won't be harmed. Did you ever hear the story of Jonah? He tried to run as well and was swallowed by a great fish. You can't escape this call."

I'd never heard of Jonah but felt a great deal of sympathy for him.

With one arm around my waist and the other holding my arm, Kupua threw both of us into the pool. Changing into an octopus, he plunged us down into the lava tubes, keeping his tentacles wrapped tight around me. His powerful grip provided sanctuary from danger but also served as a stark reminder of how truly helpless I remained, despite being chosen as queen. At the mercy of some unknown Anela, and fate itself, I huddled behind his tentacles, grateful for a barrier between me and the world, no matter how temporary.

The tubes grew darker until I could see very little. Dread pressed down upon me. All the poor choices and mistakes I'd ever made filled my mind. Vibrations continued to pound in my head, splitting it into fragments of pain.

When we finally emerged from the water, we stood on the sandy floor of a cold, dim cavern. Light filtered in through a cloudy haze from the bowels of the cave. Water dripped from the ceiling, echoing off the walls. Smoke permeated the area, smelling of apple, cinnamon and nutmeg, reminding me of Christmas back home, a strange combination given our location. Pain continued to throb inside my head. Kupua took my hand and led me deeper into the cave.

A fiery white arch loomed in front of us. No heat emanated from the flame, but it was so bright, I could hardly stand to look at it. Kupua urged me forward, but I stopped, hesitant to pass beneath it.

"Trust me, Tessa, it's safe."

Easy for him to say; he wasn't the one about to be tested. What happened if I failed, wasn't good enough? Before this moment, I had never believed my mistakes would matter all that much, never realized I'd have to be accountable for my choices. Major wake-up call, right here, right now. Ignorance no longer an option. Shock set in, shaking me to the core.

Kupua tugged my hand as he stepped through the arch, pulling me with him. Peace washed over me as I came through to the other side, easing the pounding inside my head, stilling the vibrations. As pain receded, clarity returned, and calm serenity replaced doubts.

A narrow bridge built of pearls the size of baseballs arched over a deep crevice in the ground. Spanning at least ten feet start to finish, it stretched out, beckoning me to cross. My bare feet slid over the smooth surface as I took my first steps. I turned to find Kupua still on sand, face ablaze with worry.

"I can't cross. You have to go the rest of the way on your own."

Launching myself into his arms, I fought back tears, burying my face in his chest.

He gently stroked my hair, resting his head on top of mine. "You can do this Tessa. I believe in you."

Simple words, yet the chord they struck in my heart was anything but. He believed in me. Courage blossomed, sprouting from his belief. I released him, wiping tears from my cheeks, and turned back to the bridge. "I will do this. No turning back."

On the far side of the bridge, the cave opened into an enormous room. Torches of white flame hung from the rock walls. I stood there, alone, in silence for what felt like an eternity. The only sound, my heart thumping against my chest.

Three bright lights flickered in the center of the room. They grew larger, taking shape, all blazing white. I couldn't look directly at them, they were too bright, so I kept my face down. Their brilliance engulfed the room until nothing existed but three forms of light. Trembling, determined not to flee in fear, I stood my ground.

One of the white lights glided closer to me. A booming voice spoke, and I dropped to the ground, shoving my face into the sand. It took me a minute to realize the light had not spoken out loud—the voice was in my head.

"Do you know us, Tessa Armstrong?"

My voice was hoarse when I cried out, "No, I do not know you."

"You speak correctly, you do not know us. But we know you. The Creator has known you since the day your mother conceived you in her womb. We have been sent by him to hear your answer. We do not judge, but we serve the one who does."

I had no clue what question I was supposed to answer, so I just knelt there without saying a word, fear shaking my body.

"What is your answer, Tessa? Are you worthy?"

That was easy, I knew the answer to that question. "No, I am not worthy."

A few minutes went by as I stayed frozen on the ground.

Another light moved forward. A new voice entered my head, higher pitched than the last. "Do you confess to us that you are weak and do not have the power, on your own, to rule? Do you admit to your faults, Tessa?"

Another easy question. Was it some kind of trick? Did these things, whatever they were, really believe I wanted to be queen, that I felt entitled? The only reason I'd agreed to do this was because Kupua and the queen thought it would help them. I raised my head to respond. "Please, I have no power or ability to rule, I am weak. Give Kupua and his mother another way to save Moku-ola, I really don't want to be queen. I have lots of faults. Including bitterness toward my sister after she took care of me. She looked out for my best interests, and I repaid her with anger. She didn't deserve that. I've made so many bad decisions in my life. I don't deserve to be a queen."

"Again, you speak the truth, Tessa Armstrong."

Sorrow and regret choked me, bitter pills to swallow. Tears ran down my cheeks, leaving my eyes puffy, my nose dripping. My body shook with remorse, and I wrapped my arms around my chest, curling into a ball.

The third light moved forward. The voice from this one rumbled, deep and low, shaking me to the core. "You must pay for the wrongs you have committed. But since you are not able to pay the price, the Creator has paid it for you and forgives you. Do you accept this?"

This question was not as easy as the others. Wasn't I expected to pay the consequence of my own actions?

"I don't understand. Why don't I have to be punished? Why don't I have to pay for my mistakes?"

"The one who judges has done it for you, because you are not worthy, and because the one who judges loves you, my child. What is your answer?"

My mind worked overtime to figure out the catch in all this. How could someone I didn't even know claim to love me? What response could I possibly give? If someone sacrificed on my account, shouldn't I appreciate that sacrifice? How could I refuse it? What kind of idiot refused a gift of love? After several minutes of processing, I made my decision. "I accept, even though I don't understand." As soon as the words were out of my mouth, I felt a profound sense of relief and comfort, my body sagging as though a weight had been lifted and I could finally rest.

The voices said in unison, "Well done, child. The responsibility of queen is now yours. As the one who judges has forgiven you for your mistakes, you must now show that same love for the people of Moku-ola and all life in the sea. This is a gift to be treated with the utmost care. We will be watching."

I raised my head, and they were gone. Slowly I got to my feet, brushing the sand from my knees. I staggered back across the bridge to where Kupua waited.

My voice cracked. "What just happened?"

Kupua's face lit with joy as he pulled me into his arms. "You accepted the sacrifice made by God for you. The Anela asked for you to accept, and you did. You have been chosen."

A little unsteady, I held on to him. My life tilted on its axis.

"Tessa, every member of my family comes before the Anela sooner or later. They summoned me when I was just a boy. When the vibrations started, my mother told me to come here, but she didn't come with me, I had to face them alone, just as you did. How do you feel?"

"This might sound strange, but I feel relieved, happy, yet also like I have an anchor holding me in place. Twisting my body, I checked to see if everything was intact. "What did they do to me?"

He laughed. "Forgiveness has a way of doing that, you know. Let's get out of here."

Forgiveness? Was the simple act of being forgiven all it took to bring joy into a person's heart? If that was true, then forgiveness had the power to heal. As we swam back home, the power and simplicity of that idea weaved through my mind.

CHAPTER 12

HŌ'IKE 'ANA
REVELATION

My mother used to tell me I could never truly appreciate happiness without also having known sorrow. As Kupua and I left the cave and jumped into the water, I understood she was a wise woman.

For the first time since I'd come to Moku-ola, the water felt cold. I grabbed Kupua for reassurance. He changed into an octopus and gently squeezed me with his tentacles, both of us anxious to return home.

Violent thoughts crashed into my mind from something ahead, something waiting for us. Fear churned within me, an all-too-familiar friend. Kupua sensed the danger and stopped, pushing me back against a crevice in the wall, rocks stabbing at my shoulders.

This was bad; he wouldn't be able to let go of me to fight. I searched the wall for something I could grab and use as a weapon. My fingers found a sharp rock and pulled it loose.

Kupua sent me messages to stay still and against the wall, but I decided to ignore him. I sent my own message back that we were in this together. It was nice being able to communicate with our minds while he was not in his human form. We would have to explore this new skill further, once we were both safe.

Whatever had been waiting for us swam closer, focused on me, big surprise. My image clear in its brain.

Kupua wrapped one tentacle around my waist, and another pushed me against the wall. His other tentacles loomed out in front of him, waving back and forth in the current, tips uncurling in readiness. Without warning, a rush of water surged against my face, the metallic taste of ink filling my mouth. As I groped to discover what was going on, sandpaper skin scraped my hands. Kupua convulsed, and his mind cried out in warning. A shark clamped down on him. I fumbled wildly for a vulnerable spot. Kupua's tentacles thrashed about, making it hard to find what I was searching for. My body jerked from left to right. Something knocked me in the head, and things got fuzzy for a moment or two. Finally, I located the spot I wanted and plunged the rock into the shark's eye, pushing deep. It immediately let go of Kupua and backed off. Kupua tightened his grip on me and burst away in the opposite direction, leaving a trail of ink in our wake.

Kupua pulled us up into a pool with a gravel beach. Once my feet touched ground, I dragged him out of the water, his strength ebbing from the exertion of bringing us to safety. He changed back into human form and lay limp on the ground. His back was torn open across his shoulder blades. Blood drenched his body. We needed help. Before I could figure out what to do, the shark surfaced in the pool. I reached out with my mind for Kele, not caring who else heard me. He would know how to help Kupua.

Kele heard my SOS call and let me know he was on his way. I warned him about the shark but had no idea how he would get past it. I pulled Kupua's head into my lap, praying for a miracle. I tore off a piece of my shirt and used it to put pressure on his back. He moaned and fell back into unconsciousness. My body shook. The thought of losing Kupua made my stomach rise up into my throat. I'd lost so many people I cared about. I couldn't lose Kupua too.

An eternity passed as I sat there waiting for help to arrive. Finally, I sensed Kele close by. The shark submerged and disappeared from sight. Waves rippled through the pool. A cloud of red spread out across the surface, sending a spear through my heart at the possibility another friend might be hurt. When Kele's head popped up out of the water, relief washed over me.

"Hurry, Kele, he's hurt bad."

Kele rushed up the gravel beach and removed the cloth from Kupua's back. He pulled a mixture of green salve out of a pack he was wearing and applied it liberally to Kupua's wounds. Then he bound up the wounds with bandages and cleaned Kupua's face. He poured a drink of steaming fluid and forced it down his throat.

"What is that?"

"My mudda wuz one amazing healer, an she give me all her medical recipes. Dis one foa keep infection an fevah away. Dis also has pain killer foa help when my brah wakes up. Dis made from rare seaweed plants only found in one remote part da makai."

"Will he be okay?"

Kele looked up from his work and winked at me. "Fo'real? It take more dan dis fo keep Kupua down, he's strong."

I leaned back on my heels, exhaling. "Thanks, Kele, for coming, for risking your life to help us."

"No worries. I bring some friends along fo take care of da shark. Kay den, you two are my family, I do anything fo you." He motioned back to the pool, and I noticed Fin circling in the water. I thanked him as well, letting him know Kupua would be okay. Fin did a flip and took off for his pod.

I glanced at Kele, who was applying something green to Kupua's face. Akalei's ordeal had changed him, left him more focused and determined. Worry lines gathered around his eyes. He looked tired.

"Can we move him?"

"No, not till my brah one awake and much stronga. He has fo change in da water, and he canna do dat when he unconscious or weak. We will have to stay here fo da night."

While I didn't relish the idea of spending the night on the gravel beach, I was more concerned about Kupua getting better. "Is there anything I can do to help?"

"Kay den, try mak'im more comfortable. Dig bed in da gravel, should be sand underneath."

I used my hands to push away gravel and quickly dug out a more comfortable area for Kupua. Once Kele settled him into it on his side, we dug beds for ourselves as well. Once settled, Kele pulled some food out of his pack and shared it with me. He'd come prepared. We sat in silence. It struck me as odd that Kele was handling the situation so well, considering what had happened to Akalei. Mysterious man, Kele.

"How do you do it, Kele? How do you stay so calm and focused when you've had so many problems with the sharks?

He kept his eyes down. "Ma life belongs to da Creator. I nevah allow Moho or da sharks to define who I am. If I stay angry because of what dey do to Akalei, den I would be crazy man. Akalei wuddna want dat. She my wahine, an I love her."

"Kupua is lucky to have a friend like you." There were few people in the world that would risk their own lives for a friend. Fewer still who wouldn't seek revenge after an attack on a loved one.

Kele looked up at me and winked. "I am da one who lucky to call Kupua my brah and—"

A hoarse voice interrupted him. "The two of you are giving me a headache with all this sappy talk. Please, lighten up."

Hearing Kupua's voice lit me up, and I scrambled to his side. He took my hand and kissed it, his lips cool against my skin.

"Kupua, I was so worried about you, how are you feeling?"

"Eh, grouchy, howz you feelin'?" mocked Kele.

"I'm feeling good enough to kick you back to the sea."

"Ey, anytime, shark bait," Kele replied. But when Kupua tried to get up, Kele pushed him back down with his foot. "Brah, you need more rest. I dunna wan to take advantage of an invalid."

Kupua scowled at him. Kele got out more of the liquid he'd given Kupua earlier and made him drink it.

Kupua's nose wrinkled. "Ugh, what is this stuff?"

"Dat stuff what goin make you beddah."

When he was done, Kupua turned to me and attempted a smile. "I'm sorry about all this, Tessa."

"Don't be stupid, I'm having the time of my life. The accommodations aren't so great, but you do know how to show a girl a good time."

He laughed, and his whole body relaxed. His eyes closed, and he was asleep before he could say anything else.

"Dat stuff make you sleepy," Kele said as I watched Kupua drift off. I leaned back and thought about how much Kupua meant to me. In a short time, I'd become very attached to this guy. Losing him wasn't an option.

Sometimes the only comfort to be had is in the quiet presence of those who share your grief. I put my arm on Kele's shoulder, and he gave me a sad smile. We both leaned back and settled in for the night.

A soft chirping sound woke me. I opened my eyes and glanced over at Kele snoring on the other side of Kupua. A small blue light flickered over Kupua, the size of a butterfly, dancing just above his chest. What was it? I watched it bounce around, captivated.

Kupua continued to sleep, totally unaware of the light show happening just above him. My eyes followed the light as it moved about. There was a rhythm to its movements. The light moved away from Kupua and headed deeper into the cave. Without thinking, I got up and followed it. The color in the light was the prettiest blue I'd ever seen. The chirping sound soothed me, causing me to feel all fuzzy inside. My feet were light as feathers as I bounced along after the light, deeper and deeper into the cave. All I could think about was how pretty the light glowed. The light stopped over an area in the cave where the ground wasn't visible. Somewhere in my mind that seemed odd, but the thought wasn't stronger than the pull of the light. Just as I was about to get close enough to touch the light, a hand grabbed me and yanked backward. Then two hands were on my shoulders, shaking me.

"Tessa, snap out of it, wake up!" Fog cleared from my mind. The light vanished. Something smelled really bad.

"What happened?"

"You were almost taken by the Lua Pele." Kupua pulled me into a bear hug. He was obviously feeling much better.

"Huh? The Lua . . . what?"

"The Lua Pele," he said, slowly, as if I were a child with poor hearing.

"I heard you the first time. What is the Lua Pele? I never heard of it . . . or them . . . or whatever."

"The Lua Pele lives in the volcanos beneath the ocean floor. It uses the dancing light to lure unsuspecting victims into its lair. Since no one has ever escaped from a Lua Pele, we don't know what it does to its victims, but I am sure you would not want to find out." He was right about that.

"What does it look like?"

He shrugged his shoulders, wincing in pain. "Nobody has ever seen one. They don't come out of their lair, which is why they must lure you in."

"If you know where they live, why don't you do something about them? They are a threat, aren't they?"

"All predators are a threat, but that doesn't mean they don't serve a purpose. Even the sharks play an important role in our oceans, and we need them. We just don't know enough about the Lua Pele to understand their purpose. There are some who believe they are fallen anela who seek to destroy anything that is good."

"What is that smell?

His nose wrinkled. "My guess is . . . rotting flesh? Maybe something else. It's hard to say, there's so much we don't know about them. Remember the crater on the island? I suspected those blasts were coming from the Lua Pele. Maybe it shoots the remains of its meals out of its lair with hot blasts of air. Since I didn't know for sure, I didn't want to risk your safety. That's why I didn't want to linger around the spot."

Just as he finished this explanation, Kele came running down into the cave. He stopped short of bumping into Kupua. He gave us both a scowl.

"What you two doin' back here, do I have to save you again?"

Kupua ignored him and put his arm around me. We started walking back to the water. Kele followed. "Well, looks like you all beddah. Fasta dan usual. My medicine is very good."

Kupua looked back at Kele, worry etched in his face. "Time to go."

CHAPTER 13

MOʻI WAHINE
QUEEN

Stress and anxiety surrounded me like thick fog. Time for the crowning ceremony—time to step into the responsibilities of being queen.

Akalei waltzed in with a dress created especially for me. The royal family colors of green and deep aquamarine wove through the fabric. Backless, it draped long and tapered out from the tiny pearls circling the waist, creating a nice line to the floor, glimmering as I moved.

Queen Hiiaka hovered behind me, fussing with my hair. "I always wanted a daughter." Her voice was gentle, sincere. "Even though you are young, you are very strong, Tessa. You have proven yourself to be courageous, loyal, and caring. Moku-ola will be fortunate to have a queen such as you." She sounded so sure of herself; I wished I felt as confident as she sounded.

"I'm afraid I'll let you down." Doubt rumbled through my stomach, creating the distinct possibility I might vomit any minute.

She adjusted the sash at her waist. "During the ceremony, I will pass my power to you, and no one will be able to deny you are the new queen of Moku-ola. I was just about your age when I became queen and married Kupua's father. My mother had been queen, and I spent most of my life preparing to take on the responsibility. I remember wanting to please her, to make her proud. I'll never forget the moment I realized what it truly meant to be the queen of Moku-ola, the heaviness of so much life depending on me. It was Kupua's father that made it bearable. He reminded me all I really had to do was to love. You see, Tessa, as long as you make decisions based on love for others, your love will cover a multitude of mistakes. You can't be perfect, so don't try. All you need to do is to love. Love the Creator who made you, love your family and friends, and love the creatures who share this ocean with you. That is what it means to be queen."

I turned and wrapped my arms around her, hugging her tight against me, so grateful she was there to support me.

"Are you ready?"

My spirit settled, calming my stomach. I'd wasted so much time. Finally, I felt ready to live my life, to look toward the future and love those around me. Well, maybe not everyone around me. Moho and his sharks weren't exactly tugging at my heartstrings.

We walked into a dome-shaped room with high ceilings and a pool that took up almost the entire floor. In the center a glass platform stretched out over the water where Kupua, Mike, Kele and Akalei stood waiting for me.

Kupua wore a loose green tunic belted with pearls over matching pants. Joy lit his eyes. Kele and Akalei both wore purple, the color of honor and service to the royal family. When our eyes met, the others dipped their heads. Mike stood off to the side, his face unreadable. He'd refused to change out of the clothing he'd worn when he left the beach, a silent protest to my commitment to Moku-ola.

The queen urged me to the edge of the pool, where glass steps led to the platform. She instructed me to wait as she crossed to join Kupua. When she reached him, she turned, faced me, and spoke, spreading her arms out wide. "A new queen has been chosen for Moku-ola. A queen born of love and blessed by the Creator. She is a queen tested by the Anela and found worthy. She stands before you as Tessa Armstrong, but as she crosses the water, she will become Queen Tessa of Moku-ola. I pass the power and authority given to me by our Creator into her hands."

She motioned for me to approach her. My body shook, and tears ran down my cheeks as I took the steps that would change my life forever. Responsibility weighed heavy on my shoulders, yet I felt light with joy. When I crossed the water, Kupua handed the queen a headpiece laced with intricate patterns of mother-of-pearl, which she carefully positioned on my head. It settled into my hair, weighing little more than a feather. She fastened glowing bands on both my wrists, gifts from the Anela.

"These bands carry the authority and power given to you by our Creator. They will light your way and allow you to swim through the ocean without assistance."

Mimi and Lizzy popped up out of the water and were addressed by the queen.

"Do you both bear witness to the transfer of power and accept Tessa as the new queen?"

They barked and bobbed their heads up and down. She turned to me. "Tessa, do you pledge to protect and love the people of Moku-ola and all life in the ocean?"

"I promise to do everything in my power to protect and love all under my care." My voice wavered as emotion caught in my throat. Did my pledge extend to those who'd tried to harm my friends and me? Would I have to protect Moho?

She looked at the others, authority ringing through the air. "I present to you Queen Tessa of Moku-ola."

Kupua swept me up in his arms and kissed me. Anxieties and worries disappeared in his embrace. My life rested in the hands of the Creator, and now that I'd acknowledged my destiny, he'd unlocked the bars holding my heart hostage all these years. My spirit soared.

Once everyone had hugged me and offered congratulations, Kupua whisked me into a corner for a moment alone. He licked his lips and lowered his voice. "Tessa, we only have a few minutes before my mother takes you somewhere for the night. I need you to know how amazing you are and what a great queen you're going to be. I've waited so long for you. Tessa, I love you."

My breath caught in shock at his admission, heat flushing my cheeks. Deep within my heart, his words echoed back, acknowledging a like emotion in the recesses of my soul. "Kupua, you've changed my life forever, I'll never be the same. I love you too, and it terrifies me."

His voice rumbled deep and low. "Together we are stronger than our enemy. We have nothing to fear and everything to hope for." He wiped the tears gathering at the corners of my eyes and stepped back, releasing me. "May this night bring you peace and clarity as you start this new journey."

His hand slid behind my neck. Gently, slowly, he placed a tender kiss on my lips. As we parted he whispered, "Tonight I will dream of you." Then he turned me to face his mother, who waited by the water.

Hiiaka smiled at me, genuine affection sparkling in her eyes. "I'm going to take you to a special location for your first night as queen. It's a sanctuary for you to use when you want privacy, and for this night, it serves as a place of reflection and preparation for what is to come. It will help you prepare for what you must face in Moku-ola."

For the first time I would dive into the depths on my own, equipped to face what awaited me. Would I really be able to breath underwater? A true test of my faith beckoned, just a few steps away. Approaching the edge, I drew strength from all the love surrounding me. Without looking back, I took the plunge, Hiiaka following close behind.

Warm water welcomed me in its embrace. Floating motionless under the surface, I relished the peace of hanging suspended in the ocean with no pressure to take a breath, like being in my mother's womb.

Hiiaka swam in front of me, motioning me to follow her. She led me through another maze of lava tubes. After more twists and turns than I could remember, the tube opened up, but instead of going up to a surface area, we entered an underwater cave. Once inside the cave, we went through a hole in the ceiling and were greeted by fresh, pure air. Making the shift from water to air felt effortless, as if I'd been born to it.

We were in a tiny area facing a door. Carved on the door were the words *The Queen's Chamber.* Hiiaka turned to me. "The location of this place is known only to the king and queen. This is considered a sanctuary, a safe haven where no one else can reach you. Moho will not know about this place, so you will not be disturbed. I will send Kupua in the morning to escort you back. He will be the only other person to know the Queen's Chamber exists.

I needed a century to catalog all the new information coming at me these last few days. I nodded my head. There were no words to properly describe the turbulence in my soul.

"You must open the door."

I stepped forward and placed my hand on the rock carving. A click sounded, and it opened.

Hiiaka hugged me tight against her. "You must enter on your own. Good night, sweet daughter." She turned and left, disappearing into the ocean. Silence hung over me as I stepped across the threshold.

Glass surrounded the room, a window to the sea. Fish swam past on the other side, oblivious to my presence. I couldn't say the same; their needs and desires broadcasted clearly into my mind.

In the corner, a waterfall cascaded down into a small pool. Next to the pool stood a bed shaped like a conch shell, plush with green pillows scattered everywhere, inviting one to dive into the comfort it promised. Several cushioned chairs flanked the bed, with a small table between them, and on the table, a goblet and note. I walked over and picked up the note. It read: "Dearest Tessa, may you find the same refuge and peace in this place as I have. Love, your mother, the former Queen Hiiaka."

I turned in a circle, letting the note drop to the floor. Feeling very alone in paradise.

CHAPTER 14

IPO
SWEETHEART

L ife passed by my window, carrying on its business, unaware anything in the world had changed. But my world rocked with change; everything felt new and different. Love burst from my heart, a captive finally set free.

Pushing pillows aside, I stretched my arms and legs, willing myself to wake up. Kupua would be coming for me soon. Finally, the time to go get Rachel had arrived. It seemed like I'd been waiting forever to see her again.

Easing out of bed, I walked over to the waterfall, inspecting it more closely. Behind the falling water I spotted a door. Why hadn't I noticed it before?

Stepping behind the waterfall, I reached up and touched the door. It slowly crept open. Cautiously, I peered inside. Dust puffed off the ground, musty like the room had been closed up a very long time. Trunks lined the walls, piled on top of one another. I lifted the top of one of the trunks, and gold coins spilled out. Another revealed jewels only seen in museums or on royalty. Where had all this come from?

Farther back into the room, I discovered larger artifacts. Nautical equipment and small cannons lay scattered on the floor. Piles of guns and ammunition heaped on top each other. Large pieces of artwork and gold statues leaned against the back wall. A fortune loomed in front of me.

I sat down and opened up more trunks, discovering a diary in fairly good condition. It dated back to the early 1900s. I flipped through the pages. The diary was written by a young woman named Hazel. Hazel had been traveling with her family to meet her betrothed. She came from a royal family and felt burdened to have to marry a stranger in a foreign country. As I read her writing, sympathy blossomed for her. I could relate to her fears. I skipped to the last few entries. Hazel's ship was attacked by some sort of sea monster. Her last words were those of someone making peace with the idea her life was ending.

It's coming for us. I am thankful for the love of my family. I pray the Lord has pity on my suffering and takes my soul quickly.

Kupua chose that moment to knock. Dropping the diary, I rushed across the room and swung open the door, throwing myself into his arms.

He grunted as he caught me. "Hey, ipo, is everything okay?"

"Yes, but I'm so ready to get my sister back, so tired of being here alone."

He pushed me back and looked me over carefully. "How was your night?"

I pointed toward the waterfall. "There's a hidden room behind the water. Come, let me show you." I tugged on his hand and he followed me.

His eyes widened as he took it all in. "Where did all this come from?"

"Good question. Surely your mother knows it's here." After all, this was her secret spot. Dust tickled my nose, eliciting a sneeze.

I showed him the page I'd been reading. "This is the diary of a young woman named Hazel. Her ship was attacked by a sea monster. What do you think would attack a ship like that?"

He thought a moment. "Did you say her name was Hazel?"

"Yeah, why? Does the name mean something to you?"

"My great-grandmother's name was Hazel." We both looked at the diary.

"Do you think this might be the diary of your great-grandmother?"

"Maybe, but why is it hidden in here? Everyone knows how she came to Moku-ola; it's not a secret."

Mysteries were piling up. With care, I put the diary back in the chest. Kupua took my hand, and we retreated.

"Do sea monsters exist?" I asked him, since clearly nothing was out of the realm of possibility for me now.

"Well, there are creatures surface dwellers have mistaken for sea monsters. The giant squid have often been called sea monsters by fishermen. And there are many large sea creatures able to wreck a ship if they felt threatened or attacked. But I know of no monsters in the sense you mean." He thought for a minute then continued. "There are some legends among my people of a creature that comes out only when disturbed. The legend says it will move about in the ocean until it has destroyed whatever awakened it from its resting place. But I've never seen this thing or known anyone who has. It's hard to know what a young girl might consider a monster."

Couldn't argue with his logic. Not all monsters looked scary. Some horrified because of the havoc they created in your heart. My own personal monster still waited for me. It was time to go and find out if our plan was as good as we thought. Gently, I touched Kupua's shoulder. "Time to go."

He covered my hand with his. "We'll come back here when this is over, I promise."

When we returned, Kupua's mother was seated around the table with Kele, Akalei, and Mike, looking grim.

Hiiaka spoke first. "Moho has taken our bait. He sent out a message saying if we return Tessa to Moku-ola and I agree to marry them, he will sign a truce with Kupua and offer him sanctuary in the city."

Kupua protectively pulled me closer, his arms welcome comfort.

I frowned at her. "Isn't that what we wanted? Our plan is working, right?"

Hiiaka shook her head. "There's more. Our spies report he's put Rachel in an unknown location and has her closely guarded by sharks in case something goes wrong."

I felt like I'd been hit with a brick. Rachel wasn't safe after all. But I wasn't helpless anymore. I was queen and commanded an ocean of possibility.

"I'll demand Rachel be present for my wedding. Our plan stays in place."

They all stared at me as if I'd grown a couple of extra heads. Kupua stood up. "I agree with Tessa. Once Rachel is back in the city, we can arrange for someone to take her back to the surface. Our plan will still work."

Mike joined him. "No backing out, we've got to get Rachel, we're her only chance."

Hiiaka tilted her head and motioned to Kupua and me. "Are the two of you ready for what this will cost you?"

I wasn't sure what she meant, but Kupua seemed to understand. His mood shifted. I raised my eyebrow at him. He sighed. "She means how hard it will be for me to watch Moho prepare to marry you, to act as if you belong to him. Also, to allow you to place yourself in danger, which I'm not sure I will be able to do."

I caressed his cheek with my fingertips. He was kind and protective, a gentle man. I loved that about him. I put my mouth up to his ear and whispered, "Our plan will work. We will all be safe, and you and I will be together."

I needed to believe we would succeed. Success was my only option, because I couldn't face the alternative. Kupua pulled me aside. He leaned in and pressed his lips against mine, his arms wrapping around me protectively. His kiss felt urgent and fierce, as if it might be our last. It strengthened my resolve to ensure there would be many more. We lingered in the kiss before turning back to Hiiaka and the others. I announced, "We are ready. Let's go get my sister."

CHAPTER 15

HOʻI HOU
RETURN

Once again I stood before the door to Moku-ola, but this time as a queen, not a captive. Determination replaced uncertainty in my heart. No queasy stomach today. Head held high, I embraced the authority imparted to me in my new role.

Kupua reached for my hand, but Hiiaka stepped between us. "From here on, you must act like you cannot stand being near Kupua. You have chosen Moho. Don't forget it."

She turned her gaze to Kupua. "And you must act like she has rejected you."

I swallowed. This was going to be hard. She took my hand, and Kupua stepped back behind Kele.

Akalei put her hand on Kupua's shoulder. "Together," she said.

Fists clenched at his sides, Kupua focused on the ground. Both of us would pay an emotional price for this charade. My only consolation was the fact that Mike wouldn't have to witness it; he'd been forced to wait and join us right before the wedding through a secret entrance with the help of Rico, his presence too difficult to explain away. When the door opened, we all took a collective deep breath and walked through the entry into the queen's sitting room.

Moho waited for us inside. What once had been a brightly lit room now appeared dimmed, creating dark corners and shadows. Immediately he pulled me into his arms and hugged me. Revulsion stirred, but I acted the part and smiled at him. Kupua's support enveloped my mind and gave me strength. I pushed back from Moho and acted my heart out.

"I'm so sorry I tried to go home without telling you. I had no idea they would take me from you."

He took my face in his hands, squeezing a little too tight. "You are safe now, and my mother has agreed to marry us, that's all that matters."

I was nodding when he surprised me with a kiss. His lips pressed rough and harsh against my mouth.

Kupua exploded behind me, shouting, "Don't touch her, you monster."

Kele grabbed his arm, holding him back. Kupua's cheeks reddened with anger. It was a believable act, the conflict warring on his face visible to all. Maybe not much of an act after all.

Moho looked over my head at him and sneered. "How do you like it, Brother, now that I have something you want?"

Bile rose in the back of my mouth. I needed to do something to distract them both before this went very wrong.

"Moho," I said, bringing his attention back to me, "is it true Rachel's here?"

Surprise flitted across his face before he composed himself. "Yes, I wanted to make sure she was safe, so I brought her to a secret location for protection."

I fought the urge to roll my eyes, well aware there was no room for mistakes in this game we played. Too much hinged on Moho's buying our story. "It's important to me she is here for the wedding. I want to share my wedding day with her, she's my only family." It would be hard for him to explain a refusal. I put my hand on his face, pleading with my eyes. His resolve faded. *Score one for me.*

He took my hand. "Anything you want. She'll be here tomorrow in time for the wedding. I promise you."

With a smile plastered on my face, I forced myself to hug him. "Thank you. Tomorrow will be so special. It means the world to me to have Rachel and you by my side." *Gag.*

Kupua's thoughts roiled over me, a mixture of concern, support, anger, and frustration. He thought my acting bordered on being a little too convincing. Straining, I pushed calm words back at Kupua, reassuring him of my love. He calmed, a little.

It was in that moment Moho registered my dress and headpiece and their significance. His face clouded with disbelief and he turned his attention to his mother, his voice a snarl. "What have you done?"

Unaffected by his mood, she smiled at him. "I recognized Tessa as the chosen queen, and when she told me she agreed to marry, I saw no reason to delay transferring my power and authority to her. She is now your queen."

Moho looked back at me. "I thought you didn't want to be queen."

Okay, this was a bit more difficult to explain. My back stiffened, and I lifted my chin. "Your mother explained everything to me, and I was honored by her blessing. I thought you wanted me to be queen."

He stood there, speechless, confusion whirling in the murky depths of his eyes.

"Queen Tessa, would you like to retire to the queen's chambers now?" Hiiaka asked as she took my arm and led me to the bedroom, saying over her shoulder, "We'll meet you in the dining room in an hour. Kele, take Kupua to his quarters now." Before anyone could argue, we disappeared into the bedroom.

Hiiaka let out a breath. "Well done, Tessa, but this is a dangerous game we are playing, and you must stay alert. Moho is not a fool. Try to keep out of his reach. If he keeps flaunting his position with you, Kupua might lose control."

She was right, but keeping distance between me and Moho was going to be a challenge. She must have read my thoughts because she added, "I'll help you. Stay close."

The pillows on the bed looked inviting. I plopped down and attempted to get comfortable. Hiiaka's words sank in. There could be no mistakes now; too much was at stake.

Hiiaka said a prayer over us for strength and safety. Peace washed over me as she spoke, a reminder I was not alone.

The hour passed quickly, and we were feeling better when we made our way downstairs to the main floor. Torches lit the room, with flower garlands hanging between each pair. Soft light reflected off the floor, making it sparkle. An ache tugged at my heart. If circumstances were different, the setting would be perfect. Marriage scared me, but committing myself to Kupua ignited a different set of feelings. Thoughts of spending my life with him provided comfort, not fear.

Moho and several young men from the city waited for us. When I entered, the men looked down and bowed their heads to me. I hesitated, not sure how to respond. Hiiaka whispered to me they were waiting to pledge their loyalty and accept me as their queen. I walked up to each and held out my hand. The first man kissed my hand and said, "Queen Tessa, I am Pika, and I am honored to pledge my loyalty to you." Could I believe him? If forced to choose, would he serve me or Moho? The other two men approached and repeated the same words. Hiiaka followed closely behind me, and when I reached Moho, she positioned herself between us.

Moho was not deterred. "My queen," he said, looking at me, "I have arranged for these men to serve as your personal bodyguards until we are married. They will make sure you are safe."

More like make sure I don't go anywhere, I thought. "Am I in danger?" I asked him in a soft voice, infused with as much innocence as I could muster.

He moved in closer. "With Kupua here, I fear for you and do not want to take any chances."

Hiiaka shot him a sharp look. "Moho, do not speak of your brother in such a way. Are you breaking your word? Are you not offering him sanctuary? I grow tired of this family fighting and want peace."

Her words bounced right off him. His reaction left me cold. How horrible it must feel to have a once-loved son turn away from her. I'd be devastated if Rachel rejected me in such a way. But then it hit me with a crushing blow: I had rejected Rachel, treated her love with disregard. My heart ached for them both, and I gripped Hiiaka's hand. Truly, I had no right to judge Moho.

Moho turned his face from his mother and responded as if she were invisible. I realized the fact he responded at all was for my benefit. His words were tense. "My word is good. I will not harm Kupua, but I don't trust him either."

Unfortunately Kupua chose that moment to make his own entrance, strolling in with a huge smile on his face. He had a solid grip on his emotions, which was a relief, but I failed to notice the source of his good humor. It was only when Hiiaka poked me in the ribs and I took a second look that I saw two sea lions trailing behind him. Mimi and Lizzy, both reeking of fish, waddled happily into the room. I could see from the corner of my eye how much he was enjoying himself. He'd attracted Moho's attention as well, and he didn't seem to share Kupua's good mood.

Moho turned toward the newcomers and pointed at the sea lions. "Get those creatures out of here. They do not belong at the queen's table."

Kupua kept walking. In fact, his smile only widened as he responded.

"Why, Brother, are you forgetting it is our tradition for a new queen to accept our friends from the sea at her table as they pledge their loyalty to her? Certainly you do not wish to deny our new queen these friendships."

My admiration for him surged. His eyes landed on me, and the force of his love hit me like a hurricane, leaving me breathless. I tore away from his gaze to look at Moho, who reluctantly motioned for the two sea lions to come forward. It occurred to me Kupua had arranged his own version of bodyguards for me with these two. Mimi and Lizzy stopped directly in front of me. Lizzy opened her mouth to bark, sending the stench of fish up my nose. I pretended not to recognize her.

"What are their names?"

Hiiaka leaned over to me, winked, and announced, "Tessa, show Moho how gifted you are. Ask them yourself."

I placed a hand on each of their heads. Tonight they were focused on protecting me. Yep, Kupua had gotten me bodyguards. Everyone waited for me to say something. "This is Mimi," I said, indicating the mother, "and this is her daughter, Lizzy."

Hiiaka put a hand on my shoulder. "You have a natural way with our friends of the sea."

Moho reached out his hand to touch my face, but Lizzy intercepted it with a slippery swipe of her tongue across my cheek and his fingers. He recoiled in disgust.

I caught Kupua's smile before he turned his head. Served me right for telling her to kiss him that day on the island.

Mimi and Lizzy flanked me as we moved to sit at the table. Purple sea anemones in clear bowls lined down the center, their venomous tentacles floating in water, waiting to be fed. Polished abalone shells served as bowls, each filled to the brim with seaweed wraps. The aroma of simmering garlic reminded my stomach I hadn't eaten in a while. I positioned myself on the floor between the large sea lions. Of course that meant I couldn't see Moho, who sat next to me on the other side of Lizzy.

Kupua sat directly across from me, giving him a perfect view of both Moho and myself. Hiiaka joined me next to Mimi, and Kele sat on the other side of Kupua with Akalei. One big happy family.

Moho reached across the table and dropped bits of fish into the sea anemones' tentacles. They closed around his offerings, consuming the food. Carnivorous, beautiful, and deadly. I sensed a theme.

My human bodyguards didn't join us at the table. Pika left and was now returning with a large pail of fresh fish for the sea lions, who started clapping when they saw the food. He placed several fish on the table in front of each of them, and they barked with pleasure.

Every once in a while, Lizzy nudged me with her cold nose, and I'd balance a fish carefully on the tips of her whiskers. After proving she could hold the position for several seconds, she would toss the fish in the air and gulp it down to the thunderous approval of Mimi, who would erupt into barking and clapping of her flippers.

At one point Moho attempted to lean around in front of Lizzy to speak to me, only to find himself nose to nose with her. Every time he moved to change direction, she moved with him, mimicking his position and staring him in the eyes. There was no end to her persistence, and finally he gave up trying. I really liked my new friends.

When we finished our dinner, Kupua continued his barrage of traditions. His eyes twinkled with mischief as he stood up and announced, "Moho, is it not our custom on the new queen's first night in Moku-ola to have her sit at the sacred pool and accept the well wishes of any who are waiting to see her?"

Moho stood up as well, not to be outdone. "Yes, Kupua, it is. And it would be my honor to escort her." He held out his hand for me to accept, which Lizzy promptly placed her flipper in. His expression turned to disgust as he dropped his hand, wiping it against his pant leg.

I stood up to avoid a scene and inclined my head toward Moho. "I accept your gracious offer. Please lead the way."

He did, and we all followed him down to the sacred pool with assorted bodyguards in tow. Pika let out a grunt as Lizzy butted him with her head to win the coveted spot directly behind me.

No sign of the platform or dead bodies remained. I sat on the edge of the pool and placed my feet in the cool water as Hiiaka had instructed me. When the tiger shark appeared, I recoiled, abruptly pulling my feet out. Moho placed his hands on my shoulders and whispered in my ear. "Never fear the sharks. They will not harm you, and they pledge their loyalty to you as well. Once you have accepted this one's well wishes, I'll send him away."

A shiver of revulsion shot through me. The shark glided up to me, and I placed my hand on its back. Sandpaper skin sparked memories I'd hoped to forget. Instantly the hunger of the shark, the coldness of its heart, swept through me. Kupua was right, these were not warm fuzzy creatures. Hunting and searching for prey consumed this creature. Loyalty to Moho hung like a tenuous, fragile line, held in place only by the strength of Moho's will.

Following the shark appeared an octopus the size of a small car, who wrapped a tentacle around my leg, reminding me of the first time I met Kupua. I felt a special fondness for octopuses since meeting Kupua. Gently, I closed my fingers around the tentacle. "Wow, this one is very smart." I glanced over at Hiiaka.

She nodded in agreement. "The octopuses are very intelligent creatures. They will make excellent consultants as you learn more about your new home here. They also make efficient spies, which I will explain in greater detail to you later."

Next, Ka arrived carrying a special message. She'd found a mate and was on her way to lay eggs. I ran my hand over her smooth shell and wished her well. Following Ka came a long line of various species of fish, squid, and other creatures, until my bones ached and exhaustion set in.

Hiiaka noticed my fatigue and ended the evening. Mimi and Lizzy joined us in our room. My human bodyguards and Moho made themselves comfortable for the night outside my bedroom in the sitting room. Trust ran high around here. He'd better make good on his promise to deliver Rachel, or things were gonna get ugly. Home sweet home.

CHAPTER 16

HŪNĀ
HIDDEN SECRET

I let out a sigh of relief and plopped onto the bed. Questions brewed in my head. Time to get some answers from Hiiaka. I rolled onto my stomach and propped my head up in my hands.

"Kupua and I found something very interesting at the Queen's Chamber. A room behind the waterfall filled with chests of treasure and artifacts. The sort of things you might discover in old sunken ships. What can you tell me about this?"

She waved me to follow her. "Come, I don't want to tell this story twice, so if you want to know now, we must go to Kupua so he can hear it as well."

She took my hand and led me over to the wall with the crystal vases. She reached behind a vase and pressed, revealing a secret passageway.

"Don't worry," she assured me, "Moho doesn't know about this passage, only the king and queen are allowed to know of its existence."

"Wow, there are a lot of secrets to learn around here."

She stepped into the corridor with me closely behind her. Once we passed through the door, it closed behind us, causing me to jump.

Light filled the passageway as my wrist bands came to life, making it easy to see where we headed. Hiiaka made her way through several turns, obviously very familiar with where she was going. I made a mental note of the directions we took. With no warning, she stopped. I didn't see anything to indicate we'd reached a door. She placed her hand on the wall, and it opened.

Kupua sat, kicking back on a couch, and I rushed over to him. He swept me into his arms, his grip possessive. It felt so good to be with him and not have to pretend we weren't a couple. He raised an eyebrow at his mother. "I take it there are secret passages here as well?"

She nodded and sat across from him. "Tessa told me you found the treasure room, so I've brought her here to explain to both of you one of your new responsibilities."

We sat on the couch across from her, holding each other's hands, and waited for her to explain. Like most of the rooms in Moku-ola, Kupua's contained a pool of water, but he'd added a sandy beach sloping into his. Patterns woven into the sand suggested a guest, most likely Ka, stayed with him. Replicas of whales, dolphin, seals, and other sea life carved from driftwood hung from the ceiling, a reminder of who we all fought to protect.

"As you already know, the queen is responsible for protecting the ocean and all life that dwell here." We both nodded, anxious for her to continue. "For generations, we've watched as ships from above sink into our sea and then later others come digging up these relics and disturbing the surrounding life. When a ship sinks in an area that's not fragile, we don't mind so much, but there are some areas of the ocean devastated by this activity. Tradition and responsibility dictate every shipwreck be investigated by the queen and king. If the area might be harmed by salvagers, we remove wreckage and hide it away, as you have discovered. What we hide must never be revealed above the surface. Treasure hunters snooping around our waters are the last thing we need."

Protective feelings rose within me, launching a desire to keep Moku-ola safe from discovery. Was this how Rachel felt about me? Did a desire to protect me when our parents died drive her reactions? Kupua squeezed my hand in reassurance.

We listened as Hiiaka went on. "This responsibility has become increasingly difficult to fulfill as technology above the surface has advanced. We need to act much more quickly than in the past. Finding sunken ships has gotten easier for people on the surface. But something even more serious happened recently that I haven't shared with you until now." She looked at her son with a very intense expression. "The day your father died, he was returning from an investigation of something we have not faced before. A submarine loaded with very deadly weapons sank in a chasm, home to the Skeletor eel, a rare species. When we initially went to explore the area to make a decision about how to proceed, we discovered moving the submarine might cause the weapons to explode. That isn't even the worst of it." She began pacing. "Before he died, your father discovered the surface dwellers had set up some sort of structure surrounding the submarine and were actually living down there and keeping watch over the wreckage. As your father observed them, he overheard some of them saying they had been attacked by an unknown sea monster, and were discussing ways to set traps." She stopped her pacing and turned to face us, worry lines etching her face.

Kupua stood up and hugged her. "Mother, why have you kept this burden to yourself? You could have told me."

She wrung her hands. "Because keeping Tessa safe and establishing her here was even more important. Without Tessa, there would be no hope of dealing with this situation."

I stood up, one hand on my hip, the other against my forehead. "Let me get this straight. There's a submarine wreck with deadly weapons threatening a fragile marine site, and on top of that, there are people snooping around the area who are now being attacked by some unknown sea monster. And you think I can do something about it?" *Was she crazy? While it was flattering she had confidence in me, come on, this was absurd.* Admittedly, since arriving in Moku-ola, I'd found a whole new sense of independence, but this was pushing it.

She gave me all the force of her steely gaze. "Yes, I know you can."

I threw my hands up in frustration. Clearly, my logic was not getting through to her. I dropped back down on the couch, done trying to argue with her. After all, we still had to deal with Moho and the wedding charade. How much could one person take?

Kupua joined me on the couch and brought some sanity into the conversation by asking, "Have you had anyone monitoring the situation?"

"Of course. We have several octopuses keeping an eye on things until we are ready with a plan. They will notify us if the situation worsens or if we are in danger of being discovered." Hiiaka looked at us both. "I know this is a burden, especially now with having to deal with Moho, but it is your responsibility. When everything is resolved here, you both must go to the submarine site and decide what to do."

"What about you, aren't you going to come with us?" Surely she would help resolve this issue.

"No, it's time for you to lead and for me to step back and let you. You will not be alone. Kupua, Kele, and Akalei will all be with you."

I shook my head at her. "No, Hiiaka, I have no idea what I'm doing. Without your wisdom and guidance, I might really mess things up."

Kupua turned to face me. "Tessa, don't underestimate yourself. You're not going to mess anything up. Anyway, we're in this together, and we will figure out what to do."

I leaned against his strong body, gathering comfort from his closeness. He wrapped his arm around me and I closed my eyes. Being this close to him made me believe everything would be all right.

Hiiaka walked back toward the wall where we'd entered. "We should get back to our room, get some rest."

My arms tightened around Kupua, and he kissed my cheek. "Don't worry, ipo, our charade will be over soon."

"We found something else there," I reminded him in case he agreed with his mother that I needed to be put to bed like a child.

He winked at me. "Mother, we also found a diary in one of the treasure chests. It was the diary of a woman named Hazel. Her ship was attacked and must have sunk. Is it possible this is the same Hazel as my great-grandmother?"

"Yes, Hazel was your great-grandmother. She was a princess before your great-grandfather found her floating in the ocean. I don't know what actually happened to her ship, but your great-grandfather found her alone, floating in the ocean, and brought her to Moku-ola. His dreams led him to the spot where he found her. Like you, Kupua, he'd been born into a family with no sisters. They fell in love, and she became his queen. Having been royalty herself, she took to her responsibilities quickly. They ruled together for many years before she gave birth to my mother. They were greatly loved, and it is said she was the first to start the tradition of salvaging ships. I never knew her—she died before I was born. My mother told me stories about her though, and I have fond memories of those. Hazel came from a very powerful family, and members of her family are still in power today. Hazel was convinced her family had done something to awaken the sea monster that attacked her ship. She had nightmares about this her whole life." Hiiaka rubbed her eyes. "I haven't thought about Hazel for many years."

Moku-ola certainly had its share of intrigue. "Could a sea monster really have sunken her ship?"

Worry clouded her eyes. "Hazel believed it did. But I've never seen anything like that happen during my life."

"What happened to Hazel? How did she die?"

"No one knows. She disappeared after my grandfather died. My mother told me she and my father searched everywhere for her. There was no trace of her in the ocean. Many have speculated she returned to the surface. Some believe the sea monster came to finish what he started. All I know is she just vanished."

Vanished. Exactly what I'd done when Moho grabbed me off the beach. Left Rachel with questions unanswered, speculation, and worries, never knowing what had happened to me. I wouldn't wish such a thing on my worst enemy.

Hiiaka gently touched my shoulder. "Let's get some rest. We need to be at our best tomorrow."

Kupua wrapped his arms around me. "Everything will be okay. Tomorrow, Rachel will be home safe."

I buried my face in his chest. "I hope you're right."

Wet noses greeted me back in my room. Mimi and Lizzy each got a pat on the head before I crawled into bed. Hiiaka did the same and fell asleep right away. I wasn't so lucky. Worry gnawed at me, kept me tossing and turning. Finally, I gave up and got out of bed, hoping to stretch out my anxieties.

Pacing did nothing to help my restlessness. I decided since I obviously wasn't able to sleep, I should do some exploring. The passageway fascinated me. The button behind the vase was easy to find, and I pushed it and opened the secret door.

As I stepped into the hall, a chill went down my spine; it seemed a lot creepier entering the empty space alone. I turned the opposite direction from our route earlier. Sneaking down the hall, I heard a thump behind me and jumped. I turned to find Lizzy following and let out a shudder of relief, grateful for her company.

At the end of the hall stood a wall I could see through, just like in the Queen's Chamber. Visible on the other side was the pool leading to the family entrance. Strange, I hadn't noticed a see-through wall before when we'd arrived.

A man appeared at the pool, and I slammed back against the far wall. But there was nowhere to hide.

He didn't notice me or see through the wall at all. I waved my hands back and forth, and he didn't even bother a glance in my direction. What a perfect way for the queen to check on arrivals to her home without being noticed.

The man, whom I recognized as Pika, continued, oblivious to my presence. He hunched over a bucket at the edge of the water. Moho arrived behind him and leaned against a rock, not far from my window. I tensed, fighting the urge to jump for cover. It was unsettling having him so close. He watched the pool intently. Pika knelt beside the bucket and threw live squid into the water.

Several tiger sharks thrashed around the surface. Every once in a while, one would breach, and I'd catch a glimpse of a blunt nose and razor-sharp teeth. Tiger sharks could give a person nightmares on the best of days. Most people talked about the ferocity of the great white shark, but in my opinion, the tiger ranked top of the food chain.

I didn't envy Pika his job. Moho calmly watched as his sharks spun into a feeding frenzy. Even from behind the wall, I felt their intense hunger. Each one's thoughts focused totally on feeding. Almost blind in their obsession, they operated on instinct.

When the bucket emptied, Moho called his name, and Pika turned his back to the water to answer. One of the sharks burst through the surface and grabbed Pika by the leg. He let out a blood-curdling scream as the shark dragged him into the pool. I watched in horror as Moho did nothing, his face hard and unyielding. He stood with his arms crossed, watching the struggle. Pika thrashed, trying to escape. His blood splattered the wall as sharks tore him apart piece by piece, clouding the water with red.

A moan escaped me as the sight wrenched my heart. Moho stiffened and turned toward my window. I froze; could he have heard me? He walked over and put his hands on the wall right where I stood. One hand went over my mouth, and the other, over Lizzy's. He examined the wall carefully. After a few tense minutes, he gave up and turned back to the sharks. My body relaxed, and I let out my breath.

No sign of Pika remained except the red tint to the water. Moho sat down next to the bucket and put his legs into the pool. He moved his feet against the backs of the sharks, stroking and rubbing, his face a dark mask.

Sinking to my knees, I pressed my forehead against the wall. Disgust rolled over me. I'd underestimated his ruthlessness. Doubts about seeing my sister again tugged at the fringes of my thoughts.

Lizzy whimpered, and I stroked her head. I slid my arm around her and allowed myself to relax against her strong, warm body. Exhaustion set in. Pushing off her back, I stumbled to my feet, no longer certain of my future or if I would ever see my sister again. How was I supposed to fight such evil?

CHAPTER 17

'OHANA
FAMILY

Dread twisted knots in my stomach as I got out of the shower and sat down in front of the mirror. So many dangers threatened us, and now I truly understood what we faced. Last night served as a major wake-up call about Moho's character. If any compassion remained in him, it was buried deeper than I could reach. He would not be easy to defeat because he had nothing to lose. I, on the other hand, had everything to lose.

Lizzy lumbered over and rested her head against my leg, looking at me with her enormous eyes. Her whiskers tickled my skin, distracting me from my worries. I grabbed a comb and ran it through my wet tangle of hair. The mirror had fogged up from my shower, so I rubbed it to make sure I looked presentable. I slipped into my ceremonial dress for the second time.

A knock at my door snapped me back to reality. I hurried into the bedroom and flung open the door to find Moho standing there with my sister. A rush of relief and happiness burst through me as Rachel tackled me with her body, hugging me for all she was worth.

She smelled of home, a mixture of plumeria and lavender. At last, we were together. I glanced over her shoulder at Moho, reminding myself to smile because I was supposed to be in love with him. "Thank you."

He looked genuinely pleased, his smile reaching his eyes. Before leaving us alone, he reminded me we had less than an hour until the ceremony. I forced another smile to my lips, desperate not to give away the feelings of revulsion lingering from what I'd seen last night.

Rachel pushed me into the bedroom and closed the door. After another long hug, she stepped back. Sparks practically flew from her eyes, and her jaw tensed as she waved her finger at me. "Tell me you are not getting married to that guy. He has a lot of nerve bringing us both here against our will. I don't care if he is a prince or if this place is the Promised Land. How dare he expect you to marry him after what he's done? What's his problem?"

A giggle escaped me even though I knew she was serious. In reality the situation was precarious, but it was just so good to be with her. I took her hands and led her to the bed. "Rachel, there's a lot I need to tell you, and we don't have much time."

She stilled and went silent, clasping her hands in her lap. She sat next to me and listened to the whole story.

I told her about how Moho had kidnapped me, about finding Kupua and the queen, and about our scheme to rescue her. Finally, I'd gotten it all out, including the part where I'd turned my life over to God and been crowned.

She let out a sigh. "Wow, Sis, this is a lot to absorb. I guess it'd be hard not to believe in something greater than yourself with all you've had to face. Wish I could've been here with you."

"Tell me about it." I could tell she needed time to process everything I'd told her.

She tugged on my hair. "Are you happy?"

"I really am."

Her eyes brimmed with tears, and she pulled me into another hug. She straightened, and determination settled over her features. "Okay, first I have to get back to Mike because I'm sure he's freaking out. Then we have to figure out how you and I are going to stay in touch and set up regular visits, because I am not going to just leave you down here without some way for us to stay in contact."

I guess I'd expected some sort of shock on her part. I should have known better. Rachel considered shock a waste of time.

"Rachel, Mike's here. We've arranged a meeting place near the sacred pool. Akalei's going to show you."

Her mouth dropped open. "Mike's down here?"

"Yes. And there's something else I need to say to you. After Mom and Dad died, you took care of me, and I acted like a real jerk to you. I'm so sorry, Rachel. Sorry I didn't appreciate what you did for me and how hard it must have been. Sorry I always complained instead of helping you. I've been doing a lot of thinking down here, and I've been selfish. I want us to be friends again, the way we used to be. Can you forgive me?"

Her words came out in spurts as tears rolled down her cheeks. "Sweetie, of course I forgive you. You're my little sis, you're supposed to be a pain." She kissed my cheek.

It was such a relief to have my sister back. Despite all the dangers, my world tilted back into place with Rachel next to me. She would always be my safe zone. Every nerve in my body settled in her presence.

Hiiaka came in to escort us down for the ceremony. She handed Rachel a special dress to wear. Her dress was the same color and material as mine, but in a darker shade. Her sleeves were slit down the sides, creating a billowing effect. Hiiaka braided our hair. She interlaced mine with pearls and Rachel's with puka shells. She positioned the royal headpiece on my head and declared me ready.

Rachel and I stood for a moment, looking at our reflections in the mirror. "Wow," Rachel said, "You look like Mom."

I'd never noticed the resemblance before but had to agree I did look like our mother. Large oval eyes, with freckles sprinkled across my nose.

Rachel put her arm around me. "Mom would be very proud of you Tessa. I am too." Tears threatened to flow again. I seemed to be doing that a lot today. Rachel grabbed my hand and stood there with me in silence.

Hiiaka put her arms around us both. "Any woman would be proud to call the two of you daughter. I am so happy to welcome you both into my family." If only her *family* didn't include a psychotic killer. A weird uncle you could overlook, but a wack job who controlled sharks was kinda hard to ignore.

After we dried our tears and checked our faces, we braced ourselves to confront Moho and the battle he would wage. No way he wasn't putting up a fight. The three of us left the room unified in our shared goal of surviving the day.

As I descended the stairs to the sacred pool once again, my mood sank, darkening with each step. This time I knew what waited below. What if something went wrong? Worst-case scenarios played out in my mind. Each one ended in losing someone I loved, plummeting me into unfathomable pain.

When we reached the bottom and stepped out, I could see the whole city gathered for the celebration. A new platform spread out over the sacred pool. This one clear as glass. I inhaled the fresh scent of seawater and steeled myself.

Hiiaka, Rachel, and I held hands as we stepped onto the platform. Kupua was nowhere to be seen, but I knew he hid close by because his dark tangle of emotions weaved like tendrils through my mind.

I searched the crowd, hoping to spot him, but I couldn't see where he hid. My hand stroked the satchel he'd given me earlier, carrying gifts to be presented during the ceremony. Kele and Akalei positioned themselves next to the platform, reassuring me with their presence.

Moho stood across from us, anticipating, waiting to be called forward as king. His eyes scanning the crowd, absorbing every movement. Last night's scene with Pika flashed across my thoughts, and I suppressed a shudder, determined to maintain my calm façade.

Expectancy hung in the air. We turned and faced the crowd, which lapsed into silence. Time to find out where the allegiance of the people really fell.

Hiiaka's voice rang out. "Greetings to all the people of Moku-ola. Today is a day of celebration. This is a day for honoring our new queen: Queen Tessa." She motioned for me to step forward. I took the few steps toward her, and the crowd cheered. I blushed. I never enjoyed being the center of attention.

Where was Kupua? I really needed his strength and confidence. Another scan of the crowd provided no clue as to his whereabouts.

Hiiaka placed her hand on my shoulder. "I witness to you all," she announced, "this queen is brave and more talented than any that have come before her. Queen Tessa has been tested by the Anela and found worthy. She has been blessed by the Creator."

Another cheer erupted from the people gathered before the pool. Men, women, families, all pressed together, jockeying for the best view. Toddlers perched on their fathers' shoulders waved their arms in excitement. Small children shouted my name, jumping up and down in glee.

She raised and lowered her hands in an attempt to quiet the masses before continuing. "I have seen for myself she can hear the voices of the ocean even when on land." There were murmurs among the crowd as if this was indeed something unusual. It was strange hearing her speak about me. It was going to be hard to live up to all these expectations.

Hiiaka turned to face me. "It is our custom," she whispered in my ear, "for you to choose an ambassador at this time. A sea creature who will be your messenger in the ocean." She winked at me. "I think you have already gained the loyalty of one in particular." Her eyes went to Lizzy, who sat watching us. I smiled at her in agreement. Hiiaka turned her attention back to the crowd. "She has chosen as her ambassador this sea lion, Lizzy."

Lizzy barked and shuffled over to where we stood. When she reached us on the platform, she turned and bowed to all those gathered. At least one of us knew how to work a crowd.

Hiiaka's voice faltered, and a tremor crossed her lips before she recovered her composure. "I have transferred to Queen Tessa my power and authority, and now it is time for her to proclaim her chosen king."

Showtime. She turned to me, and I swallowed hard as my part in this charade began. I gave her a hug and turned to the crowd. Dead silence. I stretched my arms out wide. "Thank you for the warm welcome you all have given me. I am so grateful for the friendships I have made since coming to Moku-ola. It's important today to honor a brave friend who risked her life to save me. Akalei of Moku-ola became gravely injured defending me. Her bravery is a model for all of us. I ask Akalei and her partner, Kele, to join me now."

Kele and Akalei emerged and joined me on the platform.

"The loyalty of Kele and Akalei is without question. In honor of the bravery and loyalty they have shown, they will now be awarded the title of Royal Guard. Their authority will be second only to mine and my king's. I have created this new position in gratitude for friendship freely given before I was crowned queen."

I pulled out a knife from my satchel and presented it to Kele. The whale-bone handle bore a single word: *Chosen*. He bowed and accepted the gift. Next, I offered a rope braided of gold to Akalei. She took it and kissed my cheek. Another moment of total silence hung over us. When they turned and took their places beside me and Rachel, the crowd bellowed with approval. A brief glance over to Moho told me he was not happy with the gesture. I ignored him and put my arms up to quiet the crowd. It took a long time, causing heat to rise in my cheeks.

"Before naming my king, I must tell you all how I came to be here." Out of the corner of my eye, I caught Moho fuming, his face red with anger. A tiger shark circled the platform. Perspiration beaded on my forehead. Was this the same shark I'd seen rip into Pika last night? Kupua's courage folded around me, and I pulled it close.

"I was brought here by the son of your beloved Queen Hiiaka, Ka Moho-alii. At the time, I wasn't aware Ka Moho-alii was the youngest son of the queen or that he had an older brother, Kupua. Ka Moho-alii told me I was in danger. He spoke of a monster who sought to kidnap me and force me to become his queen. Indeed, I felt afraid and confused as everything was happening so fast. He brought me to your fine city, and I fell in love with Moku-ola. Moho kept telling me I wasn't safe. And in truth, he was right."

My gaze landed on Rachel. Her face radiated fierceness as she inclined her head in my direction, encouraging me on. Sweat trickled down my neck, plastering locks of loose hair to my skin. I closed my eyes and licked my lips, knowing the next few words would light the firestorm.

"Danger pursued me, but not from Kupua—the threat came from Ka Moho-alii. He has defied our Creator, and it is time to set things right."

Immediately Kupua appeared at my side, tensed to fight. I had no idea where he'd come from, but his presence steadied me. "As your queen, I renounce Moho's claim on this city. He will not be my king or yours, nor will he hold you captive to his cruelty any longer."

The crowd exploded in shouts of support. Men surged forward, roaring, "Protect the queen!"

Before I could take a breath, Moho leaped across to the platform, rage contorting his face. Kupua stepped in front of me, knife in hand. Moho landed on top of him, and they both tumbled backward.

Fear gripped me as I watched them struggle. Moho knocked the knife from Kupua's hand. Without thinking, I dove for it. Just as my fingers closed around the hilt, Moho shoved his foot into my shoulder, breaking my grip. I fell back as Kupua let out a war cry. Kele stepped between us and grabbed Moho's leg, slamming his knife down into Moho's thigh. Moho still had hold of Kupua and rolled on top of him. Kupua rammed his elbow into Moho's face with so much force, they both plunged into the pool.

Kele dove in after them. All I could see was thrashing bodies and blood clouding the water. My heart ripped in two as I turned away from the battle to save my sister. There was no time to lose, I had to get Rachel out of there.

Akalei lurched forward, Mike in tow, and grabbed Rachel by the waist. The four of us hurtled ourselves into the water. My last image before the chilly saltwater closed over my head was of a mass of people swarming the platform. We swam away from the blood and writhing bodies, toward the clear blue of the ocean.

The plan was for me to head toward Lanai with Rachel, Mike, and Akalei. Kupua had promised me the sharks wouldn't harm me, which appeared to be true, but one was following us. It focused only on tracking me.

Mimi and Lizzy appeared underneath Akalei and me. We each wrapped an arm around a sea lion's back, our other hands gripping

Mike and Rachel. Once secured, Mimi and Lizzy shot through the water like torpedoes, leaving the shark far behind in our wake. Sea lions are known for their ability to evade sharks, and these two were old pros at it. They rushed into the open ocean toward Lanai.

As we approached the surface, Moho's anger raced across my thoughts. I looked back and in the distance saw he'd joined his shark in pursuit of us. My heart sank. Kupua would not give up—if he lived. What would become of all of us if he didn't survive?

Sorrow weighed me down like a heavy stone. I needed to find Kupua, to know he lived. But he'd fought for a reason. Getting Rachel home safe was the most important thing now. Once she touched ground safely, it would be up to me to deal with Moho.

As we broke the surface, I instructed Akalei, Mimi, and Lizzy to take Rachel and Mike to the beach while I headed toward an old tanker shipwrecked offshore. Strong currents surged, threatening to pull us back out to sea. Rachel started to protest and reached for me, eyes flashing with panic. Akalei grabbed her and took off toward Lanai.

By the time I got to the ship, I still maintained a slight lead over Moho and the sharks. With my energy waning, I pulled myself up onto an old ladder and climbed aboard the rusted hull. Nails jutted out from broken boards, making it difficult to navigate. I wasted no time moving toward the bow, knowing the highest point would give me the best view of the ocean.

My breath quickened as I considered what might have happened to Kupua. Either he would be close behind or something very bad had happened.

The ship wobbled beneath my feet. Several holes lined the floor. I kept my eyes on each step, careful to place my foot on solid wood. The boat rocked, knocking me off my feet. I threw my hands out to catch my fall and landed on my side. Pulling myself up, I kept one hand against the hull for balance. The ship's bow rose up out of the water, causing me to hunch over, almost crawling to the top. When I reached the bow, I scrambled onto the bowsprit so I could see out over the water with nothing obstructing my view. Dorsal fins skimmed the ocean's surface below. Tiger sharks churned the sea, creating white froth as they whipped their tails back and forth. Great, just what I needed, more sharks. Adrenaline buzzed through my veins, every nerve on edge. Behind me, I could hear Moho pulling himself up the ladder.

My back stiffened. I was a queen, not a lost or frightened girl anymore. I closed my eyes and called to my friends in the sea. It was a general call for help, so I wasn't exactly sure who might show up.

Before I was able to figure out my next move, Moho came into view. The ledge I stood on was too high for him to reach. I looked down at him, attempting to gather my thoughts.

He spoke first. "How could you betray me? I trusted you."

The irony of his words burned my already-scorched nerves. Wounded pride prodded my response. "How can you speak of betrayal when you never gave me free will to choose to be loyal to you? You took me from the beach without my consent, then you lied to me about everything. You lied about yourself, your family, and my role in all of it. You were willing to deceive everyone, including yourself, to become king. You are the one with betrayal on your hands, not me." I felt relief getting all that off my chest, even if it wasn't smart to antagonize him further.

His eyes blazed at me. "You have no idea what it's like to watch everything being given to your brother and to be left with nothing. To always be second-best. I grew tired of never having what I wanted, so I started taking it. My royal blood gives me just as much right to be king as Kupua. Besides, he has always been weak, never willing to make the hard choices."

My vision pierced through his proud and angry exterior and

glimpsed the frightened, insecure little boy inside. He'd suffered and then built up a wall between the pain and his heart.

I softened my voice. "Moho, I do know what it's like to be a younger sibling. But you've traded love for jealousy and are not the better man for it. Instead of embracing your own gifts in the family, you chose to live a lie. But living a lie is never as good as living in the truth. Moho, please, it's not too late. Your family loves you and so does the Creator. It's up to you, Moho, but we all want you back, want to reconcile, if you will only let us."

His face twisted, and a low growl rumbled in his chest. "Save your forgiveness for someone who wants it." He launched himself against the wall, scrambling toward me, a knife gripped in his hand. I looked around frantically for options.

He spoke through clenched teeth. "If you will not be my queen, then you will not be Kupua's either."

I leaned over the edge of the bowsprit, looking into the water. The sharks were gone. Something emerged from beneath the surface, but I couldn't quite make out its form. Fear obscured its intent. My hesitation allowed Moho to climb up onto the ledge within striking distance. Sweat glistened off his skin, mingled with the smell of stale fish. His face hardened with rage. Sunlight bounced off the blade in his hand, blinding my vision. He lashed out at me, his knife slicing my throat. Searing pain spread across my neck, followed by a wet gush of blood. His arm coiled back, preparing for another strike. Red blood, my blood, stained his hands. In a split second, I saw my death reflected in his eyes. Frantically, I kicked at him, but my foot slipped on the wet wood, careening me backward over the side of the ship.

Water stung my skin as I made impact flat against the surface. Air knocked out of me, leaving me disoriented and gasping.

A large orca positioned itself underneath me, and I lay across its back. We accelerated toward shore. Kupua. Fear no longer blocking my senses, I felt his love and protection. The knot in my stomach loosened. Looking down, I saw something discoloring his back. Blood. I reached for my throat, and my hands came away covered in red. Weakness overcame me, and I fought to hang on to awareness. I called out Kupua's name, then everything went black.

CHAPTER 18

KAUHALE
A HAWAIIAN HOME

Far away, a familiar voice called my name. The voice soothed, comforted. My lips wanted to move, but the effort proved too much for me. No sound escaped. I feared the voice would go away, so I tried harder. His voice. The voice I didn't want to live without hearing. Blackness pulled me down. I tried to resist, tried to reach for him, but the blackness won out.

I woke in my bedroom in Rachel's house, on Lanai. A whimper escaped me at the realization I was safe. Tension slowly drained from my muscles. A light breeze blew in through the window, causing the curtains to dance in the air. Cool cotton sheets spread soft and light against my skin. A pair of brown eyes filled with love looked down at me.

Kupua smiled and leaned in to give me a kiss on the forehead. "Never scare me like that again."

Joy shot through me, energizing me. I tried to sit up, which I immediately realized was a mistake, as the room began to spin. Black spots dotted the fringes of my vision. Kupua placed a hand on my shoulder and forced me back down against the pillow. "No hurry to get up. The doctor wants you to stay in bed until you get stronger. You lost a lot of blood."

My throat scratched when I spoke. Words came out raspy. "What happened? Is Rachel okay? Is Moho alive?"

He laughed. "With all those questions, you must be feeling better."

I folded my arms and looked at him. "Yeah, just fantastic. Now tell me what happened."

He chuckled. "Okay, I'll tell you, but you have to promise to stay in bed."

I raised an eyebrow. "I'm not making any promises. But if you don't start talking, I'll go find someone who will."

He laughed again. "Believe me, ipo, if you try to get up, a whole lot of people will be in here holding you down, especially Mike."

"You've talked to Mike?"

"Yes, your family's been worried and is determined to keep you safe. Although I don't think Mike likes me very much."

Memories of fighting off Moho haunted me. I covered my face with my hands.

Kupua caressed my cheek with his finger, pulling my hands down a few inches. His face grew serious. "You have no idea how worried I was about you. When I spotted you on the edge of that ship . . ." He looked down and trembled. "You have to promise me you will not put yourself in danger like that again."

I dropped my hands to my lap. "You know I can't. Tell me what happened."

He sighed. "Okay. After your announcement in Moku-ola, I tackled Moho and we both went into the water. I changed into an orca. Several sharks surrounded me, keeping me busy while Moho went after you." Kupua tensed. "He's a coward to refuse to face me directly in the water. After Kele and I took care of the sharks, I chased after

Moho, but both of you had a good head start on me. By the time I caught up to you, you were perched on that bow and about to jump. If I hadn't gotten there in time, you would have died." Concern clouded his face, and I squeezed his hand for encouragement. "When you were on my back, I knew something was very wrong, so I rushed to shore. Rachel was waiting with Mike. They hurried you to the doctor. Mike still isn't sure about me, and his brother is even worse. He keeps staring at me like he's afraid I'm going to bite him or something."

Kinda the same reaction I'd had the first time I'd seen him as a crocodile. The memory brought a smile to my face. "Don't worry, Mike just takes being a big brother very seriously. He'll warm up to you. Puna, on the other hand, holds a grudge, and I'm sure he isn't happy about being knocked out and left behind."

Kupua ran his hand through his hair, frowning. "Maybe, but I don't have much patience for their questions."

I tried to turn the conversation back to *my* questions. "What happened with Moho?"

His face flushed. "When you jumped off the boat, he saw I was waiting below and did not follow you into the water. He's still out there somewhere, hiding would be my guess. We'll find him eventually."

The thought of Moho still out there, plotting to hurt us, triggered the pain in my throat.

Kupua noticed my frown and took my hand. "You have nothing to worry about. We are much stronger together than he could ever imagine." He pressed his lips against mine; soft, warm, reassuring. All my worries faded away. I basked in the warmth of his affection.

Someone cleared her throat, and Kupua straightened, realizing we were no longer alone.

Rachel and Hiiaka stood in the doorway. From Rachel's expression, it was apparent she had something to tell me. Kupua turned to face them but kept his hand in mine. I felt better when he was touching me; safer, calmer.

When Rachel had our attention, she pulled Hiiaka over to the bed, her face beaming with excitement. Before I even had to ask, she blurted out her news. "Guess what, Hiiaka's decided to stay here on Lanai with us! She's going to buy the house next door and help Mike's mom out at the store. Can you believe it?"

I sat up, clutching the sheets in panic. "No. Hiiaka, you can't stay here, I can't take care of Moku-ola by myself."

She patted my arm as if I were a child being consoled. "You won't be by yourself. You'll have Kupua, Akalei, and Kele all by your side, helping you. It's better for me to live up here. I'll be able to bring Mike and Rachel to visit you whenever they want. This makes sense. We can all communicate with each other this way."

Kupua didn't seem surprised or upset. He nodded his head. "Yes," he agreed, "it's a good idea."

Traitor. I tried a different tack. "Won't you miss Moku-ola?"

"Of course, but I will be back to visit often, and the time seems right for me to do something else now. Besides, it will be good for you to establish your own leadership without me looking over your shoulder."

"But I like you looking over my shoulder." I started hyperventilating. I needed her. She couldn't be serious.

She hugged me. "You'll do fine."

"I won't be fine. I still have a lot of questions for you."

"You and Kupua have all the knowledge you need to take care of the makai."

That was debatable, and I started to argue with her.

Kupua interrupted, directing everyone out of the room. "Tessa needs to rest now so she can get her strength back. If you keep her up, we will never get back to Moku-ola." When they left, he came back to the bed and sat down beside me. "Now, get some rest so we can go home."

"Kupua, I was trying to get an answer from your mother about what we're going to do about the submarine. Don't you want to know more about it?"

"Of course, ipo, but we have plenty of time for that. I'm more concerned that you get your strength back."

I gave up and lay back against the pillow, sinking into the down feathers. Brooding.

"Kupua. I know this sounds weird, but I feel sorry for Moho. He's so bitter, so alone. I think we need to keep reaching out to him, letting him know we care about him."

He sat quietly for a few minutes. When he spoke, his voice was barely a whisper. "You're right, but it's hard after everything he's done. I'm not sure I can."

I snuggled into the pillow, exhaustion creeping up on me. "I just remember how awful it was being torn from Rachel." My hand touched his, and I quickly drifted to sleep.

When I woke again, it was dark, and Puna was sitting next to the bed. He smiled when he saw I was awake. I rubbed my eyes. "Where's Kupua?"

His expression darkened, a frown drawing his brows together. "He's talking to his mother."

My head and throat felt better. I sat up, and the world didn't twirl. A good sign.

Puna pointed to a tray next to the bed. "You need to eat. Rachel will be on my case if I bring that tray back to her with any food left on it."

That sounded like Rachel. I set the tray on my lap and began to sample the food Rachel had prepared. Fresh pineapple, mango, and papaya. Warm breadfruit with melted butter, another one of my favorites. My stomach growled.

Puna watched me closely. He appeared to have something on his mind. "Kika, I don't like this situation. Who is this person Kupua? What do we really know about him?"

I stopped eating to eye him more closely. "Puna, just because you don't know him, doesn't mean anything. He's a good man." I stuffed another piece of breadfruit into my mouth while I waited for him to respond. He wasn't going to ruin my meal.

"You are family, kika, and it's my responsibility, as the oldest, to look out for you, to protect you. Which, by the way, is not an easy job." He glanced at me with a wry smile on his lips. "You couldn't just find a nice local boy, no-o-o-o, you had to go to the bottom of the sea and nearly get killed by one of our legends. What am I going to do about you? How am I supposed to look out for you when you do things like that?"

"I don't know, Puna, maybe you just miss having someone you can boss around."

He pulled me into a hug. "You never listen anyway."

Kupua came in to check on me. Puna turned and shot him a skeptical look then pointed at me. "If this is how you take care of her, you have a lot of improving to do. What do you have to say for yourself?"

Kupua sat down next to me and took my hand, never letting his eyes leave Puna. "You are right, Puna, and all I can say is I will give my life to protect her—although, as you know, that is a hard thing to do." He must have been listening to our conversation.

Puna evidently liked his answer because he straightened up and smiled. "Yes, you are right, so now you must shoulder that burden."

"Very funny," I replied. "We will see who ends up protecting who."

Kupua leaned over and kissed me on the cheek. "You have already saved me, ipo, so of course I owe you." I softened and kissed him back.

"Ughhh, you two," Puna whined, "putting it on a little thick, aren't you? I can't hang around if you're gonna act like that."

I waved my hand at him. "Feel free to leave if you can't handle someone being nice to me."

He kissed my forehead. "Someone better always be nice to you or he will answer to me. I will go for now. Rachel asked me to pick up some firecrackers. She says they're for a friend." He nodded to Kupua and left us alone.

The next day I got out of bed, feeling like my old self again. Kupua and I both knew what this meant. I glanced over my shoulder at him. "Time to go back."

"Only if you're ready, Tessa. I've asked an octopus friend of mine to keep an eye on the submarine, and Kele is making sure Moho doesn't get back into Moku-ola. So, we don't need to leave until you're sure."

Was I ready to leave Rachel? To truly be queen? To face everything waiting for us?

I lifted my chin, feeling strength surge through me. "I'm ready."

Kupua put a hand on my shoulder and kissed my cheek. He whispered in my ear. "This is not good-bye. You and Rachel can see each other whenever you want. My mother will make sure of that."

I squeezed his hand. "I know. I don't want to draw this out. I'll say good-bye to Rachel and Mike and meet you at the beach." I choked back tears, knowing if I didn't leave soon, I might never be able to tear myself away from Rachel.

"I'll be the one with Mimi and Lizzy." He winked at me. "Those two have been very worried about you. They're your biggest fans."

Thinking of them lightened my mood. I'd missed those two.

I packed some things from my life above the surface to take with me to my new home. Photo albums from my childhood, jewelry from my mother—a locket and a beautiful pearl ring—and my favorite books made it into the dry bag. When the bag couldn't fit another item, I walked outside where Rachel, Mike, Puna, and Hiiaka waited for me in the jeep.

Rachel sat in the back with me as Mike drove us to the beach. We held hands and spoke to each other in whispers. "Tessa, it's not going to be the same without you here. I'm going to miss you so much."

I leaned against her, tears flowing down my cheeks. Regret and longing warred with responsibility in my spirit, tearing me up inside. The pain of separation from my sister still raw. "Promise you'll come visit often."

"You can count on it, Sis. Mom and Dad would be so proud, and I know you'll make a great queen." She sobbed and put an arm around me, drawing me closer.

When we arrived at the beach, we held on to each other as we got out of the car. My knuckles turned white as I gripped her arm, not wanting to let go. Pain jabbed at my heart. Mike had a brooding look on his face and said in a husky voice, "I'm worried about you. If you need anything, you send for us, okay?"

I put a reassuring hand on his shoulder. "Don't worry, Mike, I'll be fine. But if I need you, I'll send Mimi or Lizzy, I promise."

He gave me a sad smile and wrapped me into one of his bear hugs. When he let go, I gave Rachel one last hug and turned toward the water, tipping my face to the sun to catch its warmth before diving into the cool sea. Kupua waited where the waves broke. Mimi and Lizzy darted in and out of sight farther out in the surf.

Moku-ola was my home now. Moho still lurked out there somewhere, but I knew where I belonged, what I was meant to do with my life. I joined Kupua, and together we dove into the waves.

Deep in the makai, darker emotions prowled, waiting for our return.

CHAPTER 19

KĀHIKO
ANCIENT

The chasm dropped below us, as if the floor of the ocean opened its mouth in a big yawn. Somewhere in its depths, lost in darkness, a sunken submarine balanced on a rocky ledge. Sid, my octopus escort, informed me the chasm served as a breeding ground for a rare species, Skeletor eels, confirming what Hiiaka had told Kupua and me earlier. Surface dwellers were snooping around. According to Sid, some of them were missing. Sid should know—he was the octopus Kupua had put in charge of monitoring the situation and nothing got by his notice.

Three surface dwellers were left, two males and a female. They stayed in a submergible vehicle docked near the submarine. For the last few days, a flurry of activity occurred as they searched for signs of their missing friends but kept coming up with nothing.

I bit my lip, worry gnawing at me. "Do you know what happened to the missing people?"

Sid looked at me, his brown tentacles curling around him. His thoughts were clear; no evidence could be found as to what their fate might have been. He further informed us all the activity had upset the eels living in the area, and several were sick.

I shot Kupua a frown.

He dropped his head and set his hands on his hips, a sure sign he was thinking. "How do we get these surface dwellers to leave—without harming them—so we can remove the sub from the area?"

I'd been contemplating this dilemma all week. It ate at me, keeping my stomach tied up in knots. "If we sabotage their submergible so they have to return to the surface, it might give us time to move the sub. We're going to have to leave it somewhere else close by for them to retrieve, because if it just disappears, they'll be suspicious and continue looking for it."

He turned to Sid. "Sid, if you were to insert ink into their supply tanks, they'd have to go to the surface. They couldn't do repairs down here, and it would take some time for them to figure out what was wrong and replace everything."

Sid liked his idea. Concern still nipped at me. We had no idea where the two missing people were. I'd been listening, but there was no chatter anywhere in the makai about their disappearance. Sid said the surface dwellers talked like some monster had attacked them, but that just wasn't possible. If anything from the sea posed a threat, I'd be the first to know.

Of course Moho was always a possibility. We still hadn't located his hiding spot, and who knew what he might be up to? Uncertainty formed another lump in my stomach, knotting tighter whenever I thought of him. I was pretty sure Moho wouldn't bother himself with these surface dwellers, and he definitely wouldn't be interested in saving the eels. One problem at a time.

"Okay," I told Sid, "You and the others go contaminate the tanks. We'll wait here and send out calls to the whales, who can help us move the sub once the surface dwellers leave."

At least we were going to make headway with this problem. Once Sid left, Kupua and I surfaced in a nearby cave and sat on the gravel beach. We'd camp overnight until the surface dwellers left. I laughed at myself. When had I stopped being a surface dweller?

Kupua took my hand. "Something about this isn't right."

I looked into his round, soft brown eyes and sighed. My body relaxed against his, and my head rested on his shoulder. "I agree, but can't figure out what's wrong."

He stroked my hair, combing it with his fingers. "I'd suspect Moho, but he wouldn't have any interest in this sub or these people. After we move the sub, we need to talk with the eels to find out if they saw anything. I don't like not knowing what happened to the two missing people."

He squeezed me tighter. The comfort from his embrace melted through my veins like warm chocolate.

Lizzy popped her head out of the water. I rubbed under her chin with my foot, and she shook her flipper in pleasure. "Lizzy, go call the whales. We need them to help move the sub."

She barked and dove back underwater. She took her role as ambassador very seriously. In a short time, Sid returned and reported the remaining surface dwellers were preparing to leave. We settled back, hoping for a few hours rest before getting to work.

Something cold and wet tugged on my ankle. I shook my leg, rising to consciousness through a foggy haze. It squeezed harder, jolting me upright, scanning for a threat. Kupua jerked up at the same time, poised to fight the unknown intruder.

Sid released us from his slippery tentacles, sorry he'd startled us.

The surface dwellers were gone, having taken their submersible for repairs. Time to get the sub moved. Kupua and I inspected the submarine more closely. He changed into an octopus so he could maneuver around the tight spaces of the sub.

The reports were true; the sub was loaded with bombs. Moving it would be a very delicate operation.

The song of the humpbacks announced their arrival. Howls, cries and whistles vibrated through the ocean's microphone. Gliding through the water, their flukes gently propelling them forward, they greeted us. Six in all, three adult females, each with a young calf. The oldest, Adaline, suggested they work together to lift the sub so it could be moved without jarring the bombs too much. Still risky, but I agreed it would work.

As they set to the task, Kupua and I moved back against the side of the chasm, waiting to question the eels.

The eels hid in their burrows, reluctant to emerge. We searched up and down the wall of the chasm but couldn't find any willing to come out and speak to us. Their fear oozed across my skin, causing goose bumps to break out on my arms.

"They're afraid of something," I told Kupua as we looked in yet another empty hole along the wall. "What could have them so spooked?"

Before he could answer, I picked up a sound coming from below. I looked down. The chasm was so deep, the bottom wasn't visible. Nothing but darkness beneath us, sending shivers down my spine. A creature took shelter down there. Kupua edged closer to me and wrapped a tentacle around my leg, squeezing. Whatever hid below seemed confused and disoriented, like it had just woken up from a long sleep. My own fear quaked through my bones.

Kupua pulled me against the rocks, wrapping his tentacles around my waist protectively. His brain quivered with worry for our safety. Should I be afraid? No creature in the sea could harm me, so why was Kupua acting so strangely? I glanced up to check on the progress of the whales. The sub finally free of the chasm, they were gently setting it far enough away from the eels to avoid any further disruptions. Hopefully when the humans returned, they'd remove it altogether from the ocean.

I pointed down, wanting to go deeper. We needed to figure out what hid down there. He shook his head no and held me tighter. I started to argue, but thoughts from the creature intensified. It hungered. Something prodded it, but I couldn't get a clear picture of what. Maybe the creature wasn't sure. I tried to communicate directly with it, asking its name. No response. The question confused it more. Odd, I'd never met any creature of the sea who didn't know its name. Images made no sense to the creature. It didn't understand me, had never seen a human before.

It surged toward light. Instinctively I threw my hands against the rocks and braced myself. It headed our way. Since I had no idea what was coming, I commanded the whales to leave the area immediately. It wouldn't help matters if anyone got hurt. I sent out a warning to Lizzy and instructed her to return to Moku-ola. She grumbled but obeyed.

Kupua and I peered downward. Slowly, a form emerged from the dark, filling up the entire chasm, wall to wall. I held my breath, waiting.

A mouth ascended into view, with teeth the length of my body. An eye watched me as it passed, its rough body scraping against my legs as it advanced toward the edge of the chasm. Tension vibrated through my body as the creature swam past us up and out of the hole. Whales looked like guppies next to this thing. It reminded me of pictures I'd seen as a child of dinosaurs living in the sea millions of year ago. What was one doing alive and well, swimming out of a hole?

Once clear of the chasm, the creature flicked its tail and rocketed out of sight. Kupua released his grip on me and immediately changed into an orca. He definitely felt threatened. Nothing preyed on the orca except humans. At least none before this thing showed up. I climbed on his back, and he sped to Moku-ola in record time.

CHAPTER 20

POHIHIHI MYSTERY

"I'm fine," I told Kele for about the hundredth time. He hovered over me, examining every inch of my body like a worried mother.

"Tessa, I shouldha ben wit' you. You are lolo, crazy."

I ignored him and looked at Kupua. "What was that thing anyway?"

He clenched his teeth. "I'm not sure, but it doesn't belong here. We're going to have to hunt it down and kill it." For someone charged with protecting sea life, this was a strong statement.

"Kupua—"

He pulled me to him, squeezing until I could barely breathe. He spoke into my hair. "Tessa, I thought I was going to lose you out there. Didn't you hear its thoughts? This thing is focused on destruction, ready to kill anything in its path. We can't allow it to destroy other life here. We must kill it."

Protectiveness jolted through me. I wasn't sure if it came from Kupua or me, but it swamped my senses.

I whispered into his chest, "But I should be able to control it if it lives in the sea."

"I'm not so sure. It may not be controllable."

If I couldn't control it, then it posed a danger to all of us. I pulled back and looked him in the eye. Whatever we faced, we would do it together. Together we were much stronger than alone. But that didn't mean I agreed the creature needed to be destroyed, at least not until we understood what had brought it here. Too many missing pieces in this puzzle remained. "Kupua, we've got to find out why this creature is here and where it came from. What's its intent? What if there are more?"

He nodded and turned his head toward Kele. "Go check with our spies, see what they know, and report back before dinner." He kissed my forehead. "Remember, Tessa, we have guests coming."

I'd forgotten. Once a week I hosted a different family from Moku-ola for dinner as a way to get to know everyone in the village. Fast becoming a hugely popular event, my dinner parties were sought-after invitations. Tonight I'd finally meet the family who made the clothing I so admired. While I knew the actual formula for making the clothing water repellent remained a family secret, I couldn't help being excited about meeting such a creative family.

I kissed Kupua on the cheek and retreated to my bedroom to prepare for dinner. Once inside, I spotted Lizzy lounging in the water surrounding the bed. She barked a greeting. I gave her a hug, kissing her nose with enthusiasm now that she was home safe. Unfortunately I had to send her out on another dangerous errand.

"Lizzy, I need you to warn all our friends in the ocean about a monster fish on the loose. Tell everyone to be careful, because I don't know if I can control this thing." She whimpered. I stroked her head. "Please be careful, I don't want anything to happen to you."

I felt her love and dedication. She dove down into the water. I watched her go and said a silent prayer to the Creator for her safety.

I crawled onto my bed, closed my eyes, and retreated to my thoughts. Reaching out, trying to sense the monster fish. A quick search of the ocean revealed anxiety pervaded the water. Everyone buzzed nervously with news of the threat. Fish and mammals were on high alert. Lizzy was doing her job.

An unfamiliar thought pattern stood out from the general chatter: confused, tangled, without focus. The monster fish, but this time I caught more detail.

Visions of a very different ocean flashed across the screen of my mind. Abundant life teeming everywhere. Sea anemones the size of a house lined the sea floor. A Mauisaurus darted through the thoughts of the monster, its long neck and tail propelling it forward to escape a threat. The monster searched for familiar prey but found none. Confusion distorted his perception. No fear, only consuming hunger and a command to destroy.

I bolted upright. My throat choked with dread, memories of sixth-grade science class coming back to haunt me. I scrambled out of bed and ran to Kupua's room and pounded on his door.

He opened the door, wet hair clinging to his neck and face. "What's wrong?"

"I know what the monster is, what we're dealing with."

He motioned me into the room.

I paced back and forth, wringing my hands. "It's a Megalodon. A prehistoric shark. You were right, this thing is hunting and will destroy anything in its path. Kupua, we won't be able to control the creature, but I fear someone else can."

CHAPTER 21

PONO DUTY

Candles flickered on the dining table in the main room, casting bouncing shadows along its surface. Our cooks had outdone themselves, providing more food than an army could eat.

Hupo and Loli wouldn't reveal their secret for making waterproof clothing but were happy to share the story of how they'd started their business. Soon, we all chatted as easily as old friends. Their daughter, Eka, however, didn't say a word. She sat at the end of the table, looking sullen and picking at her food, her face scrunched in a permanent frown, her short brown curls in wild disarray around her face.

Kupua turned the conversation to Donnie, as we now called the Megalodon. "Be very careful when you go out into the ocean"—He leaned forward, placing his hands on the table. "There's a monster shark on the loose."

Surprisingly, this subject sparked life into Eka. Her head jerked up and her eyes brightened. "Just because it's a shark, doesn't mean it's a killer."

Her parents looked like they'd been jabbed with an electric eel.

"Eka, Kupua's just trying to warn us. Why are you being so rude?" Hupo admonished her.

"Please," I jumped in, not wanting the dinner to turn into a family argument, "Eka's right, all creatures are important. We just don't know enough about this fish and are worried for everyone. Eka's reminded us all life deserves our respect. Thank you, Eka."

She glared at me before going back to picking at her food. Unease pricked the edges of my consciousness. What tormented her so?

Once everyone left, Kupua and I sat looking out over the city.

He scratched his head. "What do you think is wrong with Eka?"

"I have no idea, but something's eating at her." I chewed on my nails, frustrated I couldn't connect with Eka. "Did you see her eyes when she talked about the shark? It was like she was on fire."

He shrugged. "Maybe she's angry about being on lockdown. It's not often one of our children grow unhappy here, but maybe she's thinking about leaving. Some do move to the surface."

Unease stabbed at me again. "Maybe, but it wasn't restlessness in her eyes, it was something stronger. What would make her so angry?"

Kele came running up to us. He hunched over, gasping, catching his breath.

Kupua frowned. "You're late with your report."

"Brah," Kele wheezed, "why you gettin' so cranky?"

Kupua shot me a grin before returning his gaze to Kele, scowl back in place. We waited while Kele caught his breath.

He straightened, setting his hands on his hips. "Da monstah is at da sub, brah. He came round me." He shook his head. "Dat is one scary fish. An . . . even worse, da surface dwellers are back in da makai, snooping around da sub. Dey no spot our Donnie yet, but I nervous dat will happen soon. Sid been tryin' to keep da water murky by having da manta rays stir up da bottom, but dat won't keep da monstah from goin' crazy."

Kupua grabbed my hand and squeezed. We knew very little about Donnie except he now threatened surface dwellers and their efforts to get the sub out of the water. Kupua's thoughts blared at me; he wanted to remove the threat as quickly as possible. I knew we still were missing something, weren't seeing the whole picture.

"Kupua, we can't kill this thing until we know how it got here and who's responsible. Whoever unleashed it is the bigger threat; we have to find out what's going on."

He released my hand and rubbed his head. "What do you have in mind?"

"This might sound crazy, but I think we should start with your great-grandmother, Hazel. Remember, her diary spoke of a sea monster. Maybe she saw it, wrote something that might help us."

His hands dropped to his lap. When he spoke, his voice sounded weary. "It's worth a try."

Kupua didn't easily get overwhelmed. Was I adding too much pressure by searching for more information? I turned my attention to Kele. "Tell Sid to keep monitoring the situation until we get there. He's to continue with the distractions for now. As soon as we have more information, we'll join you. Send out a warning to the people of Moku-ola— no one is to go out into the ocean. I'm placing the city on lockdown."

Kele nodded. "Kay den." And he took off to deliver my message.

Kupua and I returned to the Queen's Chamber to retrieve Hazel's diary. I needed to know if the monster that attacked Hazel's ship was connected to our Donnie. Her diary held our only link to the past.

Upon entering, I spun around, absorbing the view of the ocean. Peace settled over me, much like the last time I'd visited the room.

Kupua smiled and tugged my ponytail. "Have I told you today how much I love you?"

I cocked my head at him, placing my finger against my lips. "Hmmm . . . you must have forgotten."

He huffed and wrapped an arm around my shoulder. "I doubt it." He leaned in to kiss me.

I pushed him back, laughing, and walked toward the hidden room, chiding him over my shoulder, "No time for goofing around, we have work to do."

He chuckled. "Oh, with you there's always something to do: Shark attacks, sunken submarines, rescue operations, monsters. What's a guy have to do to get some downtime?"

I shook my head. "Guess you got the wrong girl."

His smiled faded, and he caught my arm. "Never say that, not even as a joke. You're exactly the right girl."

I turned toward him, placing my hand behind his neck. "And you are exactly the right guy for me too." His love cocooned me, soaking into every fiber of my being, setting my heart ablaze.

He bumped his forehead against mine. I tilted back my head, and he kissed me softly. His lips warm and reassuring. I pushed his hair back from his face and smiled at him. "Okay, now let's go check out that diary."

He stepped back, and I opened the door to the secret room. Dust stirred, causing me to sneeze. I covered my nose, holding out my wristband to light the darkness. The trunk stood right where I'd left it, and I pulled out Hazel's diary.

Hazel's ship had been attacked by some sort of sea monster. I looked more carefully at her entries leading up to the ship's demise.

June 10: Father is playing the flute; it's such a beautiful sound. He is somewhere up on deck, but I can hear the melody in my cabin, tucked warmly in my bed.

June 11: Had dinner at the captain's table with my parents. After dinner, I heard Father and the captain arguing in the captain's study.

Before Mother caught me, I heard the captain say Father had endangered everyone. This does not make sense—what could Father possibly do to endanger the ship?

Kupua and I looked at each other. "Keep reading," he urged.

June 12: Father is missing. Mother and I have searched everywhere but cannot find him. When we went through his business trunk, we found the flute he'd been playing. I tried to play it, but no sound came out. There are strange engravings along the side and some words written in a language neither of us recognized. Mother is crying a lot, and the captain has sent out a message for help.

June 14: Father is still missing. Some people on board the ship said they saw a large fish off the port side. I went to look but saw nothing. There is a great deal of tension among the passengers. Oh no, have to go.

Something attacked the ship. I felt it. I am so afraid.

Closing the diary, I set it back in the trunk, looking at the collection of items surrounding us. "Let's look to see if the flute is in one of these trunks."

We searched all the trunks, which revealed lots of interesting artifacts, but no flute.

Kupua dropped the lid on the last one. "Tessa, you should get back and check in with Kele. I want to consult with Sid and get an update on the situation at the sub. We can meet back at Moku-ola in two hours."

I whipped my head around. "I'm not sure I like that plan. We should stick together. I'll go with you."

He avoided my gaze and bit the inside of his cheek. "I can travel much faster and avoid detection better alone. If you come, we'll be much more visible and too close to the monster shark for my comfort."

I looked at my feet and let out a sigh. His worry for me wrapped around my heart. He wanted to keep me as far from Donnie as possible. Maybe he was right. "Do you always have to make so much sense?"

"Yeah." He looked relieved I'd agreed. But I didn't share the feeling. Kupua was protecting me from danger—but who was going to protect *him*?

CHAPTER 22

HŪPŌ
FOOLISH

A note waited for me on the table in my sitting room. Kele was nowhere to be found. Mumbling to myself in frustration at not finding anyone at home, I opened the letter and sat on the couch to read it.

> Dearest Queen Tessa,
> Please forgive me for being rude at dinner. I would like to make it up by sharing a family secret with you. Meet me in Shadow's Cave. I'm there waiting for you right now.
> Eka

Strange. Why would Eka want to meet outside the city? Surely she knew about the lockdown? Of course, I knew firsthand risk-taking had its own attractions. Recklessness never stopped me. Her secret didn't really interest me, but I worried about her safety and figured I better go get her before she stumbled into the path of our monster. I scribbled a note to Kupua on the back of the letter, letting him know where I'd gone.

Shadow's Cave seemed an odd choice for a meeting place. Its entrance stood not far from the city, but it was known as a place to collect a specific plant used for cooking. Maybe its proximity was why Eka chose the spot. When I arrived at the gravel beach, Eka wasn't waiting. Closing my eyes, I tried to pick up her thoughts.

Strong arms grabbed me from behind and shoved a hood over my head. I kicked at my attacker, panicked my senses hadn't warned me. Rope bound my wrists, burning against my skin. Something struck me across the back of the head. Darkness narrowed the edges of my vision as my head flopped back against a hard chest. My stomach threatened to upheave its contents as every muscle went slack. Sounds faded, muffled, as I dropped off the edge of consciousness. Finally, everything went black.

Pounding pain penetrated my consciousness, forcing me awake. Something smelled awful, a mixture of sewage and rotting flesh. The only light in the room emanated from my wristbands. No pools of water anywhere. Evidently, whoever had captured me didn't have a clue I could contact others without being in water. In one corner, a hole opened up in the floor. The smell seemed to be coming from the hole.

A manacle chaffed my ankle, chaining me to the wall farthest from the hole—which suited me just fine; the farther the better. I pushed my thoughts out toward Kupua, calling for help, telling him I was chained. Tension bombarded me. Anxiety plagued Kupua, driving him toward me. I hoped he was close. Just when I thought things couldn't get much worse, the door creaked and opened. My body tensed.

Moho stepped out from behind the door. Eka followed him, but she ventured no further than the doorway. Moho strutted toward me, stopping just out of my reach.

I rose to my feet. "I should have known it was you. Really, Moho, if you wanted to talk to me, you could have just asked. I would have come on my own."

He smiled, but his eyes blazed with anger. "I don't want to talk to you, Tessa. You are only bait for my trap. It's time Kupua went to visit the Lua Pele." He moved quickly and grabbed both my arms, shoving me against the rock wall. My shoulders struck the hard, jagged edges, and I felt my flesh tear. His hand coiled back to strike. At the last minute, I ducked and his fist slammed into the rock. He released me and doubled over, holding his hand, cursing under his breath. I scrambled as far away as my chains allowed.

He stood up, scowled at me, and tromped out of the room without saying a word. I wrapped my arms around my legs, drawing myself into a tight ball, and proceeded to sob myself to sleep.

When I woke, a cup of water and bowl of food sat next to me. My stomach growled, so I reached for the bowl and gulped down the food. I needed my strength.

The smell hadn't improved. As I contemplated whether the hole in my dungeon might serve as an escape route, a small light darted out from it. I'd seen the light before and realized this was the entrance to the Lua Pele's lair. I leaned my head against my knees. Just great. No one ever went into the lair of Lua Pele and lived to talk about it. So much for my escape plan.

The light bounced around my head. It didn't have the same mesmerizing effect on me as the last time I'd seen it. *Why?* I wondered. The last time the light had shown itself, I'd felt compelled to follow it. No such compulsion bothered me this time. Of course, chains held me in place.

The door opened again. This time Eka entered alone. Her expression suggested she wasn't in a happy kind of mood. No problem; neither was I. She stopped just out of my reach. Every muscle in her body twitched, and her hands clenched into fists.

"He loves me, you know."

"If you're referring to Moho, I highly doubt he's capable of loving anyone right now. Eka, you know he's turned away from our Creator, and until he comes back, he won't know how to love."

Her face turned red. My heart broke for her, compassion outweighing my frustration at being deceived.

Her voice rose to a shout. "You don't understand him, you don't know anything. You'll never have him, I won't allow it."

I groaned. *Seriously?* "Listen, I have absolutely no interest in Moho. I want him to come back to his family, to be forgiven. Right now, all I care about is getting out of here."

Eka laughed. "You won't be getting out of here. Moho is the true king, and I plan on being his queen."

Just as she spoke those words, Moho burst in, his face red and bulging. He grabbed Eka by the arm. "What are you doing in here? I told you to stay out of this room."

Eka started to cry. Moho pushed her toward the door and spun to face me.

Kupua crashed in behind him, pinning him against the wall, hands wrapped around his neck. Relief surged through me at seeing Kupua, knowing I no longer stood alone against Moho.

Eka inched her way toward them, careful to stay out of my reach. I yanked on the chain binding my leg, but it wouldn't budge.

Moho pushed Kupua off, using his fist to knock Kupua back a few steps.

Kupua missed the Lua Pele hole by just a step. I shrieked. Moho charged at him, but Kupua ducked, using his body weight to knock Moho's feet out from under him.

This time, Eka shrieked and dove toward Moho to block him from falling into the Lua Pele's lair. Their bodies became tangled, sending both of them tumbling into the hole. Shock was stamped on Moho's face, as he fell headfirst.

I cried out and strained forward, but the chain wrenched me to a stop.

Kupua lunged at Moho, attempting to grab his leg, but it was too late. Moho's foot disappeared over the side of the hole a split second before Kupua reached him. Eka frantically grabbed at the far edge as Moho's body pulled her down, but her fingers found no purchase on the smooth rock. Screams echoed, growing quieter the farther they fell, until silence hung over the room. Moho and Eka were gone. Kupua and I stared in shock, certain this was not what Moho had planned; his pride and overconfidence was the true weight causing his fall.

Kupua turned and met my eyes. "Are you okay?"

I nodded, speechless. He crawled over and pulled me into his arms. My body wasn't hurt, but my soul wouldn't be the same. I sobbed against his shoulder. Moho and Eka lost to the Lua Pele; it felt surreal. Their loss weighed on my heart. What would we tell Eka's parents? She was their only child, the love of their lives. The news of her loss would devastate them. I knew full well how hard it was to recover from the hole the death of a loved one left in your heart. But an only child? That would be the Grand Canyon of holes. Was there any coming back from such a loss?

CHAPTER 23

'OHE KANI
THE FLUTE

Searching the cave might not be fun, but we didn't have a choice. With Moho gone, we had to find out everything we could about what he'd been doing, whether he had anything to do with the monster shark. I plugged my nose and tried not to gag. Any information about Donnie we might find would be well worth tolerating the stench a little longer. We rifled through several cavernous rooms until we found a suspicious section of wall where the rock was smooth and polished.

Kupua ran his hands along the wall, but nothing happened. I reached up too, placing my hand against the rock, and it vibrated. Part of the wall slid to the side, revealing a dark, cold, hidden space. Our wristbands lit up, and we stepped inside.

The small closet was empty except for a shallow pool of water. A small chest lay on the bottom of the pool. A brightly colored snake covered with rings of orange, yellow, and black curled around the chest. The snake's head rested on top of the box. Its tail twitched.

The snake made no respond to my attempts to communicate. I

frowned. "Why won't it talk to me? It's clearly not dead. What's wrong with it?"

Kupua furrowed his brow in concentration, dropping his head and setting his hands on his hips. "There's something unnatural about this snake." He looked at me and shrugged. "Only one way to find out."

Before I could protest, Kupua slipped his hand into the pool and instantly changed into an exact copy of the snake. Water shimmered as he circled the snake. A yellow mist drifted off the snake's skin, creating a murky cloud.

My thoughts screamed at Kupua to get out of the water. Instead of retreating, he struck at the snake, attempting to sink his fangs directly behind the creature's head. His bite didn't find flesh. His jaws clamped shut as the snake's body dissipated into yellow mist. Kupua faltered, seemingly drugged by the mist, his body falling limp. He sank to the bottom.

I reached my arm into the pool to pull him out. As soon as water touched my skin, my arm went numb. I gasped, and my chest tightened. We didn't have much time. Before I lost total feeling, I grabbed both Kupua and the box, using my feet to push us away from the pool.

Once free of the water, Kupua didn't change back into human form, a bad sign. His body lay heavy and motionless, floppy as a rubber snake. Using my good hand, I wrapped his body around my paralyzed wrist and hugged him close to my chest, fighting off the despair pressing down on my heart. He had to survive. We needed help, fast. The numbness spread through my body. I felt it creeping into my legs, sending tingling spikes through my veins. Soon, escape wouldn't be possible. I called for help, but no one responded.

I tucked the box under my droopy arm, wrapping my belt around them both to secure it in place. I tried to stand, but my legs wouldn't respond, so I flipped onto my stomach and began scooting forward using my good hand as leverage. Progress was slow, too slow. Numbness seeped up my working arm until it became useless as well. Blackness crept around the edges of my vision. Realizing my efforts were not going to be enough, I began to pray to the Creator for help. I needed a miracle.

Before succumbing to the sleep threatening to overtake me, I heard voices in the distance, mumbled conversation stirring in the background of my awareness. I laid my head against the cool rock and relinquished consciousness to the power of sleep.

Two worried faces hovered over me. Rachel and Kele. My lips wouldn't move, and despite my efforts, no sound came from my throat. Frantically, I scanned the room for Kupua, but he was nowhere. Why wasn't he here with me? The urge to scream out my questions felt unbearable. I lay trapped in my own body.

Rachel tucked the blanket around my lifeless form. "Kele, how much longer until this wears off?"

Kele shook his head. "Dunno, she can open her eyes now." He looked directly at me. "Tessa, you an Kupua paralyzed by some sort of poison. You talk soon, 'kay? Da effect is wearin' off you sooner dan Kupua. You da bomb, 'kay," he added after seeing the panic in my eyes. "Kupua is good, no worries."

My body relaxed. Kele left, and Rachel sat on the bed.

"Hey, little sis, you had me worried, but now I know you're okay, I kinda like the idea you can't talk back at me. Gives me a chance to say a few things." She ignored me as I rolled my eyes. "First, and I know this sounds just like Mom, but, why has it been so long since I've heard from you? You promised to stay in touch, but if this is your idea of staying in touch, we have some work to do. It's not like I can just pick up a phone and call you. No-o-o-o, I have to wait for some sea animal to bring a message. The least you could do is send Lizzy every other day or so." She took a breath before starting again. "Second, are you crazy? Why would you take such a risk without backup? You had us all going nuts with worry, and if you think I'm bad, wait until Puna gets hold of you. He's been stomping around since you two arrived." Rachel paused and squeezed my hand. "You know we all love you, Tessa, that's all."

I blinked at her. Deep down, I knew she was right. I'd taken a risk, and it was foolish to have done it with so many people counting on me. Next time, I would have to be more cautious, think things through a little better.

Voices in the next room caught our attention; someone was shouting. Rachel got up and ran out. My arms and legs remained dead weight, but feeling had started to return to my fingers, so I wiggled them, trying to force my body to move. Puna's voice rose above the others, but I couldn't make out what he was saying. It felt like forever before I could hear Kele and Rachel trying to calm him down. Then some stomping and everything went quiet again. Why didn't someone come in to tell me what was going on? Finally, Rachel did return, followed by Puna, who wore a scowl on his face. They sat down on either side of me.

Puna spoke first. "Kika, I'm sorry, but it was my duty as your older brother to let Kupua know how he let us all down by putting you in such danger."

I opened my mouth and found I could whisper. "Puna, He didn't put me in danger, I did that all on my own. I'm sorry for worrying all of you. Next time we will be more careful, I promise." His scowl softened, and he leaned down to give me a kiss on the cheek. "You are forgiven, little kika."

Rachel patted my arm. "Come on, Puna, let her have some rest."

I watched them leave, frustrated I couldn't follow.

The feeling in my legs slowly returned. I kicked the blankets off.

Akalei popped her head around the door. My eyes widened; was the whole city here?

"Hey, Tessa."

"Hey back."

She came closer and sat on the bed. "Next time, how about you bring me with you. You know how I like to save your life. I'm kinda mad I didn't get to this time." She gave me her brightest smile, but she didn't fool me as she fiddled with my blanket, smoothing out the wrinkles.

"Ha-ha." I snorted and dug my heels into the mattress to push myself upright. Akalei grabbed my arm, stabilizing me. I squeezed her hand before settling back against the headboard. "Have you seen Kupua?"

She avoided my gaze. "Yes. He's not awake yet."

Her answer did nothing to help my mood. "Help me out of this bed. I want to see him."

"Tessa, you need to rest, get your strength back. Wait until he wakes up, then go see him."

"Help me or not, I'm getting out of this bed and checking on Kupua." Leaning forward, I swung my legs off the bed, pausing to allow the lightheadedness pass.

Akalei stood up. "Fine, but Kele is not going to be happy about this." She wrapped her arm around me, and I leaned into her, putting weight on my legs.

"Kele will have to deal." When I stood up, black dots checkered the edges of my vision, causing me to pause while adjusting to this new upright position.

When we entered Kupua's room, and I saw him lying motionless on the bed, my heart tightened. Kupua's chest barely moved as he breathed. Kele looked up from his vigil at Kupua's side and smiled encouragingly. "He be fine, he just got mo' of da poison dan you."

His words didn't comfort me, but when I got closer, I saw Kupua's eyes were open and tracking me. I picked up his hand and sat next to him. Our eyes held each other's gaze, communicating all the unspoken emotions we both felt. His mind reached out to mine, and we basked in each other's love. Finally, I felt relief, knowing he really was going to be okay. He reminded me of the box and wondered where it was. The question was barely across my lips when Kele pulled it out from under the bed.

Carvings along the sides of the box created grooves in the smooth, polished wood. I traced my fingers over the symbols, and the box popped open. There must be some hidden mechanism I couldn't see. I looked at Kupua, Akalei, and Kele, who were all watching intently. We'd paid a high price to recover this box, and now it was time to find out if our efforts were worth it. I lifted the lid, and a soft melody began to play.

Inside, set on plush black velvet, lay a silver flute.

CHAPTER 24

HANA ACTION

There really is no place like home. The sweet smell of Moku-ola filled my lungs, and I exhaled in joy. Kupua rested on the couch, recovering from the trip home. Shape-shifting had been difficult with his strength still limited.

We knew very little about the flute. Ongoing discussion among the four of us centered on whether we should attempt to play it. I thought we should. The others were more cautious. Meanwhile, Moku-ola remained on lockdown, and rumors were flying about sightings of Donnie.

Eka's family had gone into mourning, and the mood of the city remained dark and depressed. Pacing back and forth around the room, biting my nails, I decided enough was enough; it was time for some action. I pulled out the flute and rolled it across my palm, speculating about the possibility it held the answer to our Donnie problem. Butterflies fluttered around in my stomach as I asked myself what we were waiting for. Flute in hand, I strode down to the sacred pool with Lizzy in tow and jumped in.

Before my feet hit the water, Kupua called out to me. When I surfaced, he had already reached the pool. "Don't think for a minute you're going to go out without me," he said, as he knelt next to the water. "We agreed we're in this together, that we're stronger together, so what do you think you're doing?"

Akalei followed right behind him with a me-too look in her eye.

Kele brought up the rear, arms crossed and a frown on his face.

I held onto the side of the pool, braced for a debate about the logic of my actions. I knew they wanted me to discuss my strategy before acting, but the responsibility of the city lay on my shoulders. I was queen, and all the people of Moku-ola depended on me to keep them safe. No matter how much my friends supported me, it was my head the crown rested upon, and doing nothing wasn't an option. "Kupua, the time for waiting is over. The mood of the city grows darker, and the people cannot stay shut up much longer. It's time for action. No more discussion."

He shook his head and dove into the pool, changing into an orca. Akalei and Kele plunged in next. Wow, no argument. Emotions choked me as I realized this was an act of acceptance, of respecting my role as their queen.

I gave Akalei and Kele a slight nod of my head and swung my leg over Kupua's back, riding out of the city into the open ocean with Akalei holding on behind me. Kele grabbed a fin to glide beside us. Lizzy trailed behind, clearly happy Kupua had joined our little adventure. Her thoughts of relief buzzed around in my head so loudly, I had to focus on pushing them out to concentrate on the task at hand.

Time to search for Donnie. Kupua circled the city in wider and wider perimeters until we had traveled many miles away. No sign of Donnie. As we searched, Fin approached us and reported his pod had no news of our monster shark either. Donnie had vanished.

None of us were ready to give up. We expanded our search farther and farther out into the ocean. With all eyes in the ocean at our disposal, there was sure to be a Donnie sighting somewhere.

It wasn't until Kupua surfaced that I realized we'd arrived at the island I'd trained on before becoming queen, the island with the Lua Pele dumping ground. So remote it remained undiscovered by humans, it lay somewhere between Hawaii and Japan.

Taking a break sounded good; I was ready to sit and soak up some sunshine. Tilting my head back, I closed my eyes and figured it was as good a time as any to once again suggest playing the flute.

Once we'd all settled on the sand, I pulled out the slender silver instrument.

"I think it's time to try playing this thing."

Akalei put one hand on my arm and the other over Kele's mouth to stop him from speaking. "I'm with you Tessa, let's do it."

Kupua, sitting on the other side of me, shot Kele a frown. "I agree. Play it, Tessa."

I lifted it to my mouth, but some invisible force pushed it away. After several attempts, I dropped it into my lap and let out a sigh. "What is going on with this thing?"

Kupua picked it up, examining it closely. "Weird. Why can't you even get it to your lips? It should play when out of water, that's how the diary described my great-great-grandfather using it."

"Why can't *I* play it?"

Kupua ran his hand over the smooth silver surface. "I don't know, maybe it will only play for certain people, or in certain places. If it really does have some effect on the monster like we suspect, maybe it has properties we don't understand."

Akalei chimed in, "If this monster shark is evil, maybe only people with evil intent can play it."

She had a point.

Kupua handed the flute back to me. He got up and held out his hand. "Let's walk around the island, maybe something will come to us."

"Couldn't hurt, I guess," I said as I took his hand and tucked the flute in my pocket. We followed the path into the jungle and started jogging. It had been too long since I'd had a good run, and every muscle in my neck and shoulders knotted into balls of tension. Anxiety boiled inside me until I felt like a simmering teapot without a spout, searching for release. A soft breeze blew through my hair, and stress melted off my shoulders. Kupua and Akalei flanked me with Kele behind us, running with abandon through the trees. My senses absorbed everything: birds chirping above me, the smell of plumeria flowers, the cool saltiness of the breeze. It was heaven. None of us said a word as we cruised up and over fallen trees, through small streams, and finally stopped near a waterfall.

I leaned forward, hands on my knees, to catch my breath and noticed something in the sand. I pointed to catch Kupua's attention. Fresh footprints. I straightened. "Who else knows about this island?"

Kupua dropped to one knee to measure the print against the size of his hand. "Only my family—my mother, my brother, and Kele and Akalei, of course."

"Well, since we know your mother hasn't been here recently, someone has obviously discovered the place."

Kupua looked at me, rolled his eyes, and started following the tracks. They led away from the waterfall to a more desolate area of the island. Trees gave way to rocks as we continued to follow where the tracks led. The Lua Pele hole couldn't be far.

Sure enough, bones and other debris began to litter the path. The tracks ended at the mouth of the volcanic crater. As we stood there, the ground vibrated. Kupua grabbed my hand and yanked me back a few steps. Hot air and bits of bone spewed from the opening, raining down on the ground around us. We jumped back far enough to avoid being hit but not far enough to escape the putrid smell that followed. With his hand covering his nose, Kupua said, "I don't think we should linger here. There's nothing more we can learn."

Akalei stepped up next to me, taking my other hand. "I agree with Kupua. Let's get out of here."

"Yeah, dis place is creepy." Kele tugged Akalei's arm, trying to nudge us all back a few paces. I stood firm.

"No, there has to be some sign of why someone would be so close to the Lua Pele. It may be important." I inched closer to the opening, pulling them with me, checking the ground along the way. "Whoever has been here came barefoot, which means they might be from Moku-ola." I looked at Kupua. "Why would anyone from Moku-ola come here without our knowledge?"

Kupua shook his head, examining the ground with me. "Not for any good reason."

"You got that right," said a voice behind us. Before I had a chance to turn and see who was speaking, something hit me across the back of the head, knocking me to my knees. The all-too-familiar black dots edged out my vision. For a split second I thought, *Are you kidding me?* Around me, chaos erupted.

CHAPTER 25

PŪʻIWA
SURPRISE

The sun hung low in the sky, casting long shadows across the rocks. How much time had I lost? Turning my head to the other side to look around sent stabs of pain shooting through my skull. Okay, not gonna move. *Where was everyone?* I felt my pocket, searching for the flute . . . gone. No big surprise there. What I couldn't figure out was where Kupua, Kele, and Akalei had disappeared to. They wouldn't abandon me.

Somewhere behind me, the faint sound of sobbing disturbed the silence. I rolled onto my stomach, ignoring the protest coming from the back of my head. Still no sign of anyone, but the sobbing continued. It seemed to be coming from the Lua Pele hole. Sweat trickled down my face, and I wiped my clammy hands across my shirt. Slowly, I inched forward, sulfur burning my nostrils. Fragments of rock and bone bit into my skin as I scooted closer to the hole. I held my breath and peered over the edge. Nothing but darkness, but the sobbing got louder, clearly coming from somewhere inside.

"Is someone down there?" I called out, my voice pinging off the rock floor not too far below. The sobbing paused.

"Yes. Help me, oh please, help me!" It sounded like a young girl.

"Hold on, I'll try to get something to pull you up with." I looked around and grabbed on to some palm bark. I braided the bark together to form a makeshift rope, fumbling in my rush to finish before something happened to the girl trapped below. It would have to do.

"Hurry," the girl called out, her voice rising with agitation.

I dropped the end of the bark into the hole. "Grab on to this." I felt a tug and dug in my heels. Luckily, she didn't weigh much. With some effort, I heaved until her hands emerged through the hole and grabbed the edge. I snagged her wrists and yanked. She burst out, rolling onto her side, and looked up at me.

My breath caught. "Eka, what are you doing here?" Heat rose in my face, all the anger I'd felt at her betrayal returning.

Tears rolled down her face. Her voice trembled. "Trying to survive."

I sat back and took a deep breath, grinding out my words. "You're safe now, but you're gonna have to tell me what's going on. A lot of lives are at stake, Eka."

She sat up, keeping her face down, avoiding my eyes. "I feel so ashamed." Covered in soot, she smelled like she'd been in a Dumpster. My heart softened toward her; I couldn't imagine what she'd been through down in that hole.

"Eka, no matter what you've done, you know the Creator will forgive you. I forgive you too, but you have to tell me." As my heart truly forgave Eka, the weight of bitterness lifted off my shoulders, lightening my load. I waited.

Eka sniffled. "He just left me, Queen Tessa, he just left me."

I sighed, patience not my strongest quality. "Who left you?"

She looked up. "Moho."

I raised an eyebrow at her, my stomach churning at the mention on his name. "He's still alive?"

She nodded. "Oh yeah. After we fell into the Lua Pele hole, we started following a tunnel, looking for a way out. When we got here a rope hung down within our reach. Moho climbed up first. I thought he was gonna pull me up, but he didn't. He just took the rope and laughed at me. He said I knew too much and wasn't worth the risk. I really loved him. Obviously he didn't feel the same way." She started sobbing again. I moved closer and put my arm around her. Boy, she really smelled bad.

"What was down there? Did you see the Lua Pele?"

She tensed. "No, Moho said he was protected."

"Protected? What do you mean?"

She shook her head. "I don't know, but I never saw anything. It smells really bad down there, but I couldn't see anything."

"Maybe that was lucky for you." If it was a Lua Pele hole, she was lucky to be alive. But I still needed to know more.

"Why would Moho consider you a threat?"

She took a deep breath. "I know who called the monster."

Finally, the break we needed. I squeezed her arm. "Start talking."

She picked at her fingernails. "Moho knows this man on the surface. He says he's related to royalty or something. Anyway, Moho and him made a deal. He said he could release a monster Moho could control. When Moho took back Moku-ola, he would help this guy find something in the ocean he wanted, something to make him rich." She ducked her head. "Sorry."

"What's this man's name?" Moho making friends with men from the surface couldn't be good for us. Moku-ola's very existence was at stake.

"Henry Wier."

Never heard of him. I heard voices approaching and let out a sigh of relief. "Thank you, Eka. This will help."

She took my hand. "Queen Tessa, I'm sorry. I know I messed up."

I smiled at her, brushing soot off her hair. "It's okay, Eka. Your family is going to be so happy to learn you're alive. In the future, just remember who your true friends are." True friends laid down their life to protect you, a lesson I'd learned firsthand.

Kupua, Kele, and Akalei came running up to us. They stopped when they spotted Eka. I looked up at them. "I'm guessing it was Moho who hit me?"

Kupua nodded in agreement.

I rubbed my hand over the lump forming on the back of my head, still tender to the touch. "Just once, I want to be the one to knock someone out."

Kupua knelt next to me. "He got away—with the flute."

Kele stepped closer to Eka and squatted down to look her in the eyes. "I got mo bad news. Eka, your dad swam in da makai to look fo you. He nevah believed you were dead. He found Donnie. So sorry." He bowed his head for a moment then gently touched her shoulder. "Your dad is gone."

Eka dropped her head into her hands and unleashed a heart-rending, soul-curdling scream.

CHAPTER 26

ILI
SURFACE

We formed a plan. Kele and Akalei gathered Eka between them and headed back to Moku-ola. Her distress incapacitated her ability to swim or even orient to her surroundings. Fin and his pod traveled alongside providing protection, using sonar to steer clear of any large objects such as our monster shark.

Kupua and I set out to find this Henry guy. From what Eka reported, he appeared to be the key to discovering how to deal with Donnie. I could only hope nothing else went wrong. Of course, the odds didn't seem to be in our favor.

Kupua and I started by visiting Oahu, since it's the most populated island. Our first stop: a library.

I clicked on the Internet browser as I sat at the library computer and typed in the name Henry Wier. Kupua looked over my shoulder. "Way cool."

"Yeah, let's hope this guy is in here somewhere." I crossed my fingers, knowing this was a long shot.

Twenty Henry Wiers popped up. Ughh. Who'd have thought it was such a common name? We slogged through each, looking for something to indicate the Henry Wier we searched for. I typed in Hawaii to narrow the search.

Bingo. Henry Wier, renowned treasure hunter, rose to the top of the list. After a few searches, we came up with an address. Lucky us, he lived on the island not far from us. This must be our guy. I copied down the location.

Henry's house wasn't hard to find, located right on the beach and surrounded by a ten-foot-high fence with a locked wrought-iron gate. Security cameras perched atop the gate, and an intercom blinked from a block column to my right. Not exactly low profile. Banyan trees dotted the grounds, providing shade and privacy. Knowing Wier was on Team Moho, we couldn't simply show up and expect his full cooperation. I looked at Kupua. "Now what?"

He gave me a sweet smile, showing off his dimples. "Now I make like a seagull and check out what's behind these walls. I want to know what we're facing before we announce our arrival. You wait here."

I started to argue, but he changed and lifted into the air before I got a word out. *Great.* Not knowing what he might face inside the walls churned my stomach over a few times. If this guy was working with Moho, he had to be trouble. The tide was rolling in, so I walked over to the surf, sat down, and wiggled my toes in the water, inhaling the crisp ocean air.

After a few minutes, Lizzie's head bobbed in the surf. I waved at her to come closer. She had news. She waddled onto the beach, plopped her head into my lap, and proceeded to relay her message.

Sid had an idea; he really was a brilliant octopus. Sid believed if we could find the guy who knew how to call the monster and get him to the chasm, the monster would follow. He also thought he had a way to neutralize Donnie. Nice to know Sid had so much confidence in us. Lizzie thought the plan involved the endangered eels, who had come out of hiding just to help. I instructed her to get everyone ready and promised we would do our best to show up. She planted a wet, fishy kiss on my cheek and waddled back into the surf to deliver my message. My nerves calmed; at least someone had a plan. Sid better know what he was doing.

Not too much later, Kupua landed next to me and morphed back into human form. I reached out for his hand. "So, what's the deal?"

"This guy, Henry, has lots of security around the place, and they're well armed. On the positive side, there's no sign of Moho." He gave me a grim smile. "At least we know what we're facing, sort of."

I squeezed his hand. "Let's go ring his doorbell and see what he has to say."

Of course, first we'd have to get onto the property. When we reached the iron gate, we pushed the buzzer on the intercom.

A gruff voice answered. "What do you want?"

I took the lead, hoping a female voice would be less threatening, even though I knew the cameras had homed in on us. "Aloha, could I speak with Mr. Wier, please?"

"Who's asking?"

"I'm a friend of Moho." *Well, I would be if he weren't trying to take over my city and murder my friends.* I still held out hope for him.

Silence. We waited as the owner of the gruff voice decided what to do with us.

A tall, slim man in his forties approached the gate. He wore white linen pants and a short-sleeved black silk shirt. His wavy black hair was trimmed short, and his dark eyes glinted with interest as he took in our bare feet and tangled hair. His mouth rose on one side in a half smile as he addressed us. "So, how do you know Moho?"

Kupua stepped forward, placing his body slightly in front of mine but not enough to block my view, his posture protective. "He's family. We've come to find out how you know him."

Henry laughed, a cruel, cynical sound. "I'm not inclined to speak with total strangers about my private business. Why don't you tell me what you are doing here, and we'll go from there."

Kupua's muscles flexed. "Can we speak in private?"

"Listen, you aren't getting through this gate until I know a lot more about who you are and what you want." A burly security guard stepped up to the gate and pointed his shotgun in our direction. This guy wasn't messing around.

Kupua looked at me over his shoulder. We both knew we couldn't reveal anything about Moku-ola without jeopardizing the safety of our people. We had no idea what Moho had already revealed to Henry. I moved closer to the iron gate, wrapping my hand around one of the bars. "Mr. Weir, we're here because a friend told us you have a special flute that might help us with a shark problem we're experiencing."

Henry's face twisted into an ugly sneer. "This conversation is over." He turned and walked out of sight, leaving us alone with the guard and his gun.

The guard banged the muzzle of his weapon against the gate. "You heard him, get out of here, and I recommend you don't come back."

He got no argument from us. We retreated to the beach, plopping down on the sand. Kupua shot me a sly look.

"During my scouting flight, I dug a hole under the fence big enough for you to slide through. If we go in at night, we have a shot at getting in unnoticed and looking around."

"We have to do more than look around. We have to get Henry to the chasm." I told him about Sid's plan.

He stretched his legs out and ran his hands through his hair. "How are we gonna pull that off?"

I burrowed my feet into the warm sand, my heart sinking as I considered our options. Now that we'd spoken with the treasure hunter, it was obvious he would never come with us willingly. Yet we had to take him to the chasm—we couldn't sit back and do nothing while Moho used Donnie to terrorize and kill our people. "Well, if we get Henry to the water, it should be easy. Is that hole big enough to drag him through with me?"

"I guess we're gonna find out."

We watched the sunset, waiting for dark. Crimson, gold, and orange hues burst across the sky. Seagulls dive-bombed into the ocean, hunting up their dinner, squawking at each other over their catches. Distant voices of families packing up for the day traveled through the breeze, accompanied by the smell of barbeques being lit. As the sun dipped below the horizon, I got up brushing the sand from my legs.

"Let's get this over with."

Kupua walked me to a far corner of the fence where he'd dug the hole. He wrapped his arm around my shoulder and leaned in, placing a kiss on my forehead. "Tessa, stay low to the ground. If anything happens, get out, don't wait for me. Promise."

I looked up into his soft brown eyes and knew I would never make that promise. "Kupua, you know I could never leave you behind. No matter what happens, we stay together."

He closed his eyes and dropped his head. "You are going to be the death of me."

I reached up and stroked his cheek. "You told me we're stronger together. We can do this."

He grasped my hand and pressed it against his lips, resting his forehead against mine. His love and strength poured into my soul, and we parted stronger than before.

I squirmed under the fence with no trouble. Kupua changed into a seagull, flew over, and waited, perched on a banyan tree. The back door appeared free of security guards. Guess they hadn't expected trouble from a seagull.

Staying low as directed, I crept up to an open window on the side of the house, waving for Kupua to do his thing. His job was to get Henry to chase him out the back door, where I would trip him and tie him up with some rope Kupua had scrounged off a surfer.

Kupua flew in, and I crept along the grass to the back of the house, hoping our luck would hold. After a few minutes, banging erupted from inside, and Kupua flew through the screen door, followed by Henry, waving his hands and cursing. I slung my foot in front of Henry, and he toppled onto the grass, landing facedown with a thud. I vaulted onto his back, grabbing his hands, but he proved too quick and powerful, tossing me off with ease. Before I knew what happened, he had me pinned to the ground, his forearm across my throat, cutting off my air. Behind him, Kupua changed back to human and punched him in the temple, causing him to keel over, out cold.

I pushed him off me and frowned at Kupua. "Now for the hard part."

We each took an end and carried Henry toward the wall. I was beginning to think this was going to work until a guard turned the corner and spotted us.

"Hey, you there," he shouted and raised his gun. My stomach dropped. Kupua immediately changed into a pelican and charged him, wings flapping, beak snapping. Floodlights clicked on, illuminating the scene. The guard freaked out. You would have thought he'd seen a ghost; he turned white as a sheet and dropped to the ground, passed out. But other voices shouted inside the house. We weren't going to be alone much longer.

I didn't waste any time. I dove under the fence, turned, and grabbed

Henry's feet to pull him after me. Kupua met me on the other side and changed back.

"That was too close. Let's get moving." We grabbed Henry and hurried down to the water. Once in the ocean, Kupua changed into an orca, positioning himself beneath us with me holding tight to Henry, my hands still shaking from the adrenaline rush from what we'd just done. We sped toward the chasm.

CHAPTER 27

HOʻOLĀLĀ
THE PLAN

Akalei intercepted us before we reached the chasm. She got right to business. "Okay, we don't have much time, here's how it's going down. Sid wants you to take Henry to the bottom of the chasm. When you get down there, the eels will show you how to reach an open-air cave where you can watch Donnie approach. Get on the beach, don't stay in the water, it won't be safe. Sid plans to lure the monster into the cave where he has a surprise." She took a breath. "I'm gonna help Kele get our surprise ready. Sorry I don't have more time to explain. Trust me." She gave me a hug and took off.

I rubbed Kupua's back with my free hand. "Let's hope Sid knows what he's doing."

The deeper we dove into the chasm, the darker it became. Kupua used his whale sonar to navigate.

"This is creepy," I said, shuddering, a chill coursing through my veins. "We must be getting close to the bottom."

I picked up the thoughts of two female eels waiting for us. One of the eels, Chang, greeted me and instructed us to follow her. Chang guided us up through a hole in the wall and into the cave. A soft green glow from the walls provided enough light to see what we were doing. Kupua and I laid Henry on the sandy beach and looked around. We were surrounded by rock walls with no tunnels leading deeper into the cave, a very cramped area. One of the walls slanted upward, transparent, allowing us to see straight up the chasm. Little flickers of light illuminated the darkness from multiple points in the chasm, like blinking Christmas lights. I wondered if the lights came from fish like the ones Akalei had shown me. Chang warned us again to stay out of the water. What was up with that? She took off and left us alone.

I tied Henry's hands with some rope Akalei left us. We didn't need him to panic when he woke up and go flailing straight into Donnie's mouth. Kupua shook him, and he started to come around, his eyelids fluttering.

He spoke before he opened his eyes. "Where am I?"

I knelt next to him, keeping my voice soft. "You are in a cave under the ocean. We don't want to hurt you, we just need your cooperation. When we're done, you'll be taken back to the surface, I promise."

He opened his eyes, rage smoldering in their depths. "Who are you?"

I smiled at him, attempting to mask my own flare of anger at the threat he and Moho posed to those I loved. "Someone you don't want to mess with, understand?"

He nodded, never dropping his glaring eyes from my face, as if memorizing every feature.

Kupua and I helped him sit up and leaned him against the cave wall. Once he was settled, I began my own questioning.

"Tell me about the deal you made with Moho."

He sneered, his eyes flashing. "I'm not telling you anything."

Kupua leaned in closer, placing his hands against the wall on either side of Henry's head. "Not the correct answer. Now, start talking . . . we don't want to hurt you."

Henry's eyes got big and his mouth dropped open, but he wasn't looking at Kupua. I turned to follow his gaze and froze. I motioned for Kupua to turn around.

Through the transparent wall, we viewed Sid careening down the chasm. Our monster shark was chasing him, close behind. What was Sid thinking? I reached out to his thoughts and picked up his focus on getting to the cave.

I grabbed Kupua's arm. "We'd better brace ourselves."

We both backed up against the wall. Donnie was gaining on Sid. I held my breath. Sid shot ink at Donnie, and things got cloudy, making it hard to see anything.

A ripple surged in the cave's pool. A tentacle popped out of the water, and I grabbed it, pulling Sid from the pool as a mouthful of teeth burst through the surface with one of Sid's tentacles gripped in its jaws. I yanked with all my strength, but the tentacle snagged on the shark's tooth. My feet slipped through the sand, and Kupua grabbed me, pulling backward. Donnie breached farther out of the water, catching my foot in the side of his jaw, slicing through skin.

Pain and panic rushed through me as I lurched backward, freeing my foot. Just then the water lit up and an electrical charge filled the air, sending tingling sparks across my skin. I heard a boom. Donnie released Sid and submerged underwater. The three of us fell back onto the sand, Sid's tentacle ripping off in the process.

I stared in horror at Sid, lifeless in my arms.

Kupua grabbed my face and turned it toward him. "Tessa, don't worry, an octopus can lose a tentacle and live; he'll be okay."

"He doesn't look okay to me." I scooted Sid back away from the edge of the water, taking no chances. Then I remembered Henry and looked over to where we had left him. He was gone.

I looked at Kupua. "What . . . where could he have gone?" The guy had just vanished into thin air. There was no trace of him. I turned back to Sid, cradling him in my arms, searching his brain for any trace of activity. Bluish blood dripped down my hand from his torn tentacle. His bravery humbled me.

As we discussed what to do with Donnie now that we had him secured, part of the wall behind us moved and a door opened. Kele and Akalei stepped through. I let out a huge sigh of relief. Akalei grabbed me and hugged me tight. "Thank the Creator you are okay."

"Back at you," I told her. "You'd better tell us what's going on."

Kele carried a big bucket of sweet-smelling water and gently lifted Sid into it. He looked at me. "Dis will help our friend get mo beddah. He take one dirty lickings."

I nodded and took Akalei's hand. "Start explaining, my friend."

"Well, the eels have temporarily immobilized our monster here with electricity. Kele and I came behind the shark with a few friends and moved a boulder behind the opening so little sharky can't get loose again. The boulder was granite and blocked the electricity from reaching us."

Sounded good to me. Akalei pointed to the door. "Our eel friends knew about some secret entrances, so we figured we could get you all out this way and avoid the sparky water."

"Okay . . . but how did Henry escape?"

She frowned. "Guess he knew some tricks as well. Hope he didn't get in the water." I hoped so too and felt responsible for his safety.

Kele motioned for us to follow him, and we trudged through the door into a tunnel. I was so ready to be out of there. But what would we do with Donnie, now that we had him trapped?

CHAPTER 28

HO'OLAULE'A
CELEBRATION

I felt vibrations thrumming beneath my feet before I heard the crowd. Everyone in Moku-ola gathered at the ceremonial pool. A melody drifted up to me, joyous singing of worship and celebration, lifting my spirit. We had a lot to celebrate, but also losses to mourn. The lockdown finally had been lifted, and once again it was safe to be out in the makai. No more monster shark on the loose. Of course, the real monster still lurked out there. No telling what trouble he might be brewing. But that could wait; everyone deserved time to rejoice, even though it tasted bittersweet. Losing Eka's father tainted the joy of removing the threat of Donnie. Sid and his eels ensured Donnie stayed in a coma-like state until we figured out what to do with him. Thinking about it made my brain hurt.

As I stepped into the open room looking out over Moku-ola, Eka nearly bowled me over. Her face red and puffy from crying, she hugged me tight. Pulling back, she went to her knees and gazed up at me, tears glistening in her eyes. "Queen Tessa, I want to pledge my loyalty to you and ask your forgiveness. I am so sorry

I deceived you. Please forgive me. I want to honor and serve you, Your Highness."

I pulled her to her feet. "You are already forgiven, Eka." I hugged her back. "I accept your pledge and give you my word I will protect you, but remember, the one you serve is the Creator."

She sobbed into my chest. "If only I hadn't gone with Moho, my dad would be alive."

I smoothed her hair and wiped her tears, her anguish piercing my heart. "Eka, we will all miss your father, but he is with the Creator now. You can honor both by how you live from now on." The truth of my words struck a chord in my own heart, steadying me with a peace I'd only recently experienced. The Creator was with me as well, providing a calm anchor in the storm of life. Never again would I have to carry grief or burdens alone. All bitterness gone, replaced with forgiveness and a certainty about who I was and the destiny I'd agreed to step into.

She gave me one last squeeze and ran to join her mother below in the crowd. I watched her scurry down the steps and hoped she could stay free of Moho's reach.

Kupua put his arm around me and kissed my cheek. "Are you still glad you accepted all this?"

I looked around the room, my heart warming at the sight of my friends, all safe. "This might sound crazy, but I've never felt more sure of anything in my life."

"Even with Moho and this Henry guy still out there to deal with and Donnie as our new pet?"

His love flowed over me, and I sent mine surging back to him, smiling up into his eyes. "Even with all that. As long as we face it together." Donnie was in good hands, and we'd figure out how to make sure he survived without hurting anyone else.

He kissed my hand, and we walked to the edge to look out at the city. Akalei and Kele joined us. Kele put his hand on Kupua's shoulder and mine. "Ho, you two is the best, garans."

Akalei rolled her eyes at him and took my hand. "He means *guaranteed*. We love you both so much."

I smiled at them, tears welling up in my eyes. "I love you too."

Lizzy nudged me, squeezing between Akalei and me, rubbing her head against my leg. I stroked her silky fur, thanking her for being so brave.

The roar of the crowd intensified. I waved, acknowledging the celebration below. A cheer rang out. The whole city lit up with colored lights. Banners hung from homes with my name proclaimed in bold letters. Even the pool was crowded with all our friends from the ocean. Sid, minus one tentacle but alive and well, hovered at the center, and I blew him a kiss.

Kupua drew me close, and I laid my head on his shoulder. Peace and joy filled my heart. No matter what lay ahead, I was right where I was supposed to be. *Mahalo*, I said in my heart to the Creator. *Thank you.*

Then God said, ". . . and rule over the fish of the sea and over the birds of the sky, and over every living thing that moves on the earth." Genesis 1:28

MAKAI QUEEN

BOOK CLUB
STUDY QUESTIONS

CHAPTERS 1-3

1. What emotional issues was Tessa struggling with?
2. How can you relate?
3. How was Tessa dealing with the stresses in her life?
4. What do you do to deal with stress?

CHAPTERS 4-6

1. How did Tessa feel when she first learned about God's plan for her life? What is it God is asking you to do that you are resisting?

CHAPTERS 7-9

1. Describe the differences between how Moho and Kupua treated Tessa. Can you think of examples from your life of young men who are either a Moho or Kupua?
2. Tessa discovers that God has given her special gifts to carry out His plan. What gifts has he given you? How are you using those gifts to glorify Him?

CHAPTERS 10-12

1. How did Tessa change after she embraced God's plan for her life?
2. What did you learn about forgiveness from Tessa?
3. Who do you need to forgive? What is the barrier to forgiving that individual?

CHAPTERS 13-15

1. As Tessa accepts the crown of Moku-ola, how does she change?
2. How have you changed, as you learn to walk in obedience to God?

CHAPTERS 16-18

1. Tessa and Rachel are reunited and Rachel supports Tessa's decision to become queen. How does it feel when a loved one supports your choices?
2. Moho does not accept forgiveness and rejects the support of his family. Describe times in your life when you have rejected your family and their support.
3. Compare and contrast Tessa's and Moho's reactions to forgiveness.

CHAPTERS 19-21

1. One of the responsibilities of the new queen is to protect and care for the ocean. What does stewardship mean for you?
2. Describe examples when you have stood up for something you believed in.

CHAPTERS 22-24

1. Why do you think Eka deceived Tessa?
2. How did Tessa respond? How do you respond when you feel betrayed?

CHAPTERS 25-28

1. What are the top three messages you took away from *Makai Queen*?
2. Who are your favorite characters and why?

PIDGEN GLOSSARY

FOB — fresh off the boat

brah / braddah — good friend

broke da mouth — good food

fo'real? — Are you serious?

grinds — food for eating

habut — mad

howzit? — Hello, how's it going?

huhu — mad

lolo — crazy

shark bait — someone who does not go in the sun, so their skin
      stays white